Praise for Sweet Healing

"If you know someone who's faced with type 2 diabetes or a degenerative metabolic health crisis, I highly recommend this inspirational novel! In *Sweet Healing*, the characters demonstrate how each small step in the process of healing builds upon the previous ones. This book inspires readers to take a proactive approach to their healing and offers innovative tips for health, happiness, and longevity."

— Marci Shimoff, #1 *New York Times* best-selling author of *Happy for No Reason*, *Love for No Reason*, and *Chicken Soup for the Woman's Soul*

"As a nation, we are suffering from the crippling effects of many chronic and degenerative diseases. Type 2 diabetes is the worst offender and the most preventable. In this page-turner, a wonderful book, Michael Bedar lays out a message of hope that includes a framework that can guide us all back to using food and movement as the most powerful tools to maintain our health and vitality. I look forward to using this as a trusted resource with all of my patients diagnosed with diabetes and other degenerative diseases."

— Harry McIlroy, MD, integrative physician

"*Sweet Healing* is a story of our time that reveals a reality that more people on Earth are beginning to experience ... where the extraordinary becomes the ordinary."

— Jia Patton, author of *Celebrate Life* and *May All Be Fed: Diet for a New World*, with John Robbins

"A powerful story about the nature of healing and healing with nature."

— Elson Haas, MD, founder of the Preventive Medical Center of Marin, author of *Eating with the Seasons*

"*Sweet Healing* rocks! It's a heck of an adventure for novel lovers; it's a tale that will touch anyone who has been affected by the epidemic of diabetes and chronic disease. As a mother, I appreciate that this book is the first tool of its type—a gripping read of fiction that will leave you inspired, motivated, and hungry for a healthier lifestyle ... Devour this book and share it with your friends now!"

— Cathy Silvers, actor from the TV sitcom *Happy Days*, author of *Happy Days, Healthy Living*, and producer of *The Healthy Living Show*

"Michael Bedar's real-life tale is a *Way of the Peaceful Warrior* and *Celestine Prophecy*–type adventure of a family's incredible journey from sickness into health and with that knowledge, teaching others how to heal themselves."

— Annie Padden Jubb, author of *LifeFood Recipe Book: Living on Life Force* and *Secrets of an Alkaline Body: The New Science of Colloidal Biology*; owner of the LifeFood Organic restaurant chain

"This book was amazing. Michael Bedar's expertise in his field of holistic healing is surpassed only by his dedication and love for serving people. *Sweet Healing* is a kaleidoscopic journey into the little-known (until now) subject of naturally recovering from type 2 diabetes. If you are diabetic or know someone who is, read this book and awaken into wellness. It just may save your life."

— Frank Ferrante, subject of the award-winning documentary *May I Be Frank* and author of the book *May I Be Frank*

"*Sweet Healing* is an empowering and inspiring evidence-based novel that benefits not only diabetics but anyone challenged by dis-ease. It is a well-researched and extremely well-written book that clearly demonstrates the value of a holistic (body-mind-spirit) approach to treating health conditions and healing one's life. Through this captivating story, Michael Bedar has beautifully presented a self-care option far beyond the world of drugs and surgery."

— Robert Ivker, DO, ABIHM, cofounder and past president, American Board of Integrative Holistic Medicine; author of the best-selling book *Sinus Survival*

"A unique and entertaining approach to getting a very important message across. You'll learn more about the personal side of diabetes and how to deal with it in this short novel than you will by reading medical documents. Well done!!"

— Mike Anderson, RaveDiet.com, writer, producer, and narrator of the documentary films *Eating* and *Healing Cancer from Inside Out*

"If you or your family are faced with the challenge of type 2 diabetes, I recommend that you read *Sweet Healing: A Whole*

Health Journey. It will take you on a possible journey to better health and a life empowered by positive choices, informed by proven research and presented as an entertaining read."

— Mike Adams, the Health Ranger, editor of NaturalNews.com, author of *Take Back Your Health Power* and *How to Halt Diabetes in 25 Days*

"A healing journey that not only touches your heart, but also your mind's eye."

— Brian Clement, PhD, NMD, LN, Director, Hippocrates Health Institute

"I had one thing missing from my formula for a vibrant and compassionate workplace—a clear understanding of the role of health in behavior and of behavior in health. The book *Sweet Healing: A Whole Health Journey* fills what was missing for me with a compelling story about spiritual nutrition. Well done, Michael Bedar!"

— Stephen C. Lundin, PhD, author of the five-million-copy best-selling *FISH! A Remarkable Way to Boost Morale and Improve Performance*

"For people searching, this book is a parable about waking up and getting your spark back par excellence! I heartily and excitedly recommend *Sweet Healing: A Whole Health Journey* as a boon to those who want to find out what's possible in the realm of their well-being. Read it on a plane, in bed, in a book club, or on your train commute. Just read it!"

— Nomi Shannon, author of *What Do Raw Fooders Eat 1 & 2*, *The Raw Gourmet*, and *Raw Food Celebrations*

"Get ready for a made-to-order inspiration sandwich that nudges you toward your goals of high-level wellness, family harmony, uplifting awareness, and *more life*. Bedar is an expert at using true, everyday human character traits in their realistic expression in fiction, to reinforce your highest vision. You'll want to get extra copies of this empowering book to give as gifts, too."

— Susan Smith Jones, PhD, author of *Walking on Air: Your 30-Day Inside and Out Rejuvenation Makeover*, *The Joy Factor: 10 Sacred Practices for Radiant Health*, and *Recipes for Health Bliss*

"*Sweet Healing* is a must-read for anyone interested in taking the path of whole-person wellness. Captivating!"

— Mike Chaet, PhD, author of *The Whole Health Warrior*; *LOOPS, LOOPS for Life*; and *The Storyteller: The Wisdom of Legend and Lore*

"This book is filled with Michael's caring and generous personality, infused with his dedication to serving and raising awareness for the world around him as if it were his own family. In this book you'll find a great story to help avail yourself of wisdom and knowledge about eating and living a healthier lifestyle. A story written like this comes from someone walking his talk. *Sweet Healing* is inspiring to those suffering with preventable and reversible illnesses, so they may create new habits and ways of living that reinforce a loving, healthy sense of self."

— Debbie Merrill, USFSA silver medalist, author of *Raw Truth to the Fountain of Youth*, host of the Debbie Merrill Show

SWEET HEALING - A WHOLE HEALTH JOURNEY

Michael Bedar

ISBN: 1505445884
ISBN 13: 9781505445886
Library of Congress Control Number: 2015905357
CreateSpace Independent Publishing Platform
North Charleston, South Carolina

Contents

Dedication

To every person who has loved enough to heal him- or herself. It is you who root this book in reality and inspire this writing.

Acknowledgments

I wish to thank many people whose support has been indispensable: my parents, David and Martina Bedar, for your steadfast presence; Jaime and Jason Jackson, for your abiding belief in me; Eleanor Feingold for being generous beyond any description; the editorial staff and project team at CreateSpace; Gabriel Cousens, MD, for the expert healing and lifestyle approaches you practice, teach, and have written about extensively, and for holding a space where I could become educated in the ways of the healing, transformative "pathless path." Thanks to Mike Chaet—without your key suggestions, the Three Foundational Principles and Seven Sacred Practices would not be in their current form, and I might not have embarked upon writing this book in the way I did. To Laura Buehning, MD, for your medical sciences review; Harry McIlroy, MD, for your valuable feedback; Leonid Afremov for your gorgeous and heartfelt paintings, including *Fog in the Park* which graces the front cover; Laurie Masters of Green Song Press for key edits; Scott Stoller and family for giving your friendship; Abe Heisler for reviewing the manuscript; Trevor Justice for sharing writing experiences; Cody Chaet for your insight and time; Annie Jubb for specific, direct feedback; Marna Schwartz for your encouragement; Dr. Aumatma Shah for blessing the time I wrote; and wellness and consciousness teachers in my life too numerable to name. My gratitude to the many storytelling guides in my life, including Dan Millman, Jean Houston, James

Redfield, Joe Jenkins, Joseph F. Girzone, A.M. Homes, and others; and to Laura Hahn, Ron Atwood, Rodolfo Esteves, Shanta Marie Buttersworth, George Lawton, Howard and Barbara Finkelstein, Katie Laughlin, Sergei Boutenko, Valya Boutenko, Patti Breitman, Diana Leotta, Greg and Patli Rohrbach, Kathy and Dale Jackson, Chris Whitcoe, Janet McKee, Steven Engle, Darlene Schule, Bernie and Eileen Slobotkin, Monique Arnon, and Iris Azoulay, for your generosity. Also, special thanks to the Tree of Life Foundation, the Cousens School of Holistic Wellness, friends of the two Tree of Life Centers of the Bay Area, the East Bay Healing Collective, the Brisbane Community, and everyone I may have omitted who encouraged and supported me as this story was conceived and birthed.

The information expressed in this book does not constitute an attempt to practice medicine nor does it establish a practitioner-patient relationship. This book is for entertainment and personal growth purposes only. Statements made in this book have not been evaluated by the U.S. Food & Drug Administration (FDA). The information provided is not intended to diagnose, treat, cure any disease or be used as the basis for treating a particular symptom or disease. Any products discussed or endorsed are not intended to diagnose, treat, cure any diseases or be used as the basis for treating a particular symptom or disease.

The information expressed in the following pages is not meant to replace you working with a physician or health care practitioner when implementing any ideas or protocol discussed throughout the book. Always seek the advice of your physician or other qualified health care practitioner with any questions you may have regarding your health or medical condition, or as it specifically relates to implementing any ideas, protocols, or suggestions discussed throughout the book.

We live in a culture that can easily trap us in malnutritious food and illness, yet there always remains a spark of the true nature in each person that can help one return to wellness and wholeness. For over forty-two years have I been in medical practice, and for twenty-three of them I have directed the Tree of Life Center US, in Patagonia, Arizona. At the Tree of Life, we offer holistic healing and spiritually activating retreats, programs, and vacation experiences in a natural, vibrant environment. Michael Bedar has served us there as a meditation teacher and healing process facilitator. Here we have witnessed a steady stream of profound health transformations among our guests who have embraced the foundational principles and practices of whole health depicted in this novel.

More than 300 million people worldwide suffer from diabetes, about 90% of these being type 2 diabetics. By age 65, nearly 27% of those who grow up in the current Western "culture-of-death" receive this diagnosis. I refer to this pandemic situation with a more accurate term, "chronic diabetes degenerative syndrome," a condition that engenders heart attacks, strokes, weakness, pain, crippling, and blindness, and that reduces life span by an average of 11 to 18 years! Collectively, that is a lot of lost time, in which parents and elders could pass on values, love, and wisdom to their children and communities. Even if we're lucky enough find out that lifestyle change can reverse disease and generate a recovery, actually transforming and healing can be a stumbling, unexpected, and sometimes awe-inspiring path.

Enter *Sweet Healing*, a riveting, unforgettable allegory which, along with my own book, *There Is a Cure for Diabetes—Second Edition*, offers a striking alternative to that losing battle, shining a light so readers can find their lost keys to natural health and life-force recovery.

As Michael's thesis advisor from 2009 to 2012 in the Cousens' School of Holistic Wellness Masters Program, I know that the story he has written is grounded in a deep understanding of what people really go through when faced with a health challenge such as type 2 diabetes, and the spillover effects of such a crisis on their families and communities. He has based the narrative on his scholarship, life experience, and guideship for others. He writes with a well-developed sense of the human condition—the essential choices people must confront, and the physical, emotional, mental, and spiritual potholes and mountaintops they will face—as they set forth down the path to health transformation. Through unpredictable turns of events, Bedar's writing makes it almost effortless for us to enjoy the way the characters face their physical, emotional, mental, and spiritual potholes and mountaintops in transforming their level of wellbeing.

You will get at least three clear-cut benefits from reading *Sweet Healing*: first, this book will move your heart—you will experience a sense of possibility that a transformative healing journey of this magnitude can indeed occur in *your own* life; and that natural vitality is available not only to yourself, but to people you'll want to share it with. Second, the story will help bring forth the calling to heal from within you, inspiring you to create and structure the enduring, vibrant life that is your birthright.

And third, you will learn practical steps, co-developed by my research, the work of Mike Chaet, Ph.D., at the Whole Health Warrior Academy, and Mr. Bedar, for cultivating the skills, healthy-living and food knowledge, emotions, attitudes, perspectives, and beliefs that allow your inner healer to "switch on."

Sweet Healing speaks to the soul's desire to find its way. It will touch your heart and remind you of all that you love, and all that you have to heal for. It contains a core parable enabling you to connect with your courage, and go in a direction towards one of your greatest treasures, your health. Be ready for insights about what blocks you in life, and be receptive to lifestyle practices you can use for whole-person health. Let this engrossing book show you the qualities that lie dormant within you, waiting to serve your own healing and well-being when awakened.

"I have set before you life and death" (Deut. 30:19).

May reading this book lead you, wherever you are today, to choose a lifelong, fulfilling path of rejuvenation and transformation, grounded in love, compassion, and inspired choices.

Rabbi Gabriel Cousens, MD, MD(H), ND(hc), DD
Director, Tree of Life Center US
Director, Cousens School of Holistic Wellness
Director and president, Tree of Life Foundation

Did I pay enough attention? Did I complete my part? I don't know—I was barely twenty at the time. Had the specialness of the opportunity dawned on me? Did I listen to the small voice guiding me to receive and carry on my father's example of compassion, strength, and humility? Did I let the day my dad's world went dark make its mark on me? And did I comprehend the value of life and understand what would grow to be my father's passion?

As I wondered, a pink ray of light shone through the wispy clouds, streamed in through the window, and outlined the white hair of the woman sitting next to me. Her aged features glowed in the late-morning sunshine. Her name was Hope.

"Mom," I got her attention gently. "Can you believe my little girls are the same age now that I was back when, well, you know…"

After a pause as though gathering her thoughts, my mother said, "As I suspect you remember, your father had a motto from the first day I met him, his battle cry and calling card. He would proclaim it in triumph at the end of every job he completed. You know, he was one good electrician. He even shouted it on the day we moved into our home in the foothills after he wired the power circuits for our own house."

"'Flipping the switch releases the power!'" I said, conjuring Dad. "That's his saying, right?"

"Yes, son, that's the one! As I grew to know your father, I realized that he wasn't just referring to the moment when he finished wiring a building and flipped on the switches that lit the lights and sent the ventilation pumps a-whirring."

"What else did he mean?" I asked.

"When you came around he was starting to get big downtown high-rise contracts, but when I met your father, he was doing electrical work for the poorest housing at the edges of town. Each time he finished a job, he'd say it proudly: 'Flipping the switch releases the power!'

"When your father and I began to get close to each other, he told me he was referring to his own personal power—his personal drive to rise out of and beyond his origins. With each switch, he was laying it on the line to build up a stronger foundation for his goals and dreams…which, fortunately, included me…and then you. Your father and I even had the vision that we would be grandparents one day. Hey, we could dream, couldn't we?"

I am closer to fifty than forty myself, married for a quarter century to my sweetheart, Dana, but I still look at my father's way of living and working with a little bit of juvenile awe and definitely man-to-man respect.

"Hey, Mom—there is one thing I haven't told a soul before, but I've been feeling like it's time to let it out." I inched toward the edge of my seat as I spoke, and I noticed my mom glance up.

I continued, "Dana and I, well, we wanted the way that Dad went through his ordeal to be alive in our lives. We wanted what he learned to help shape the way we lived, and how our kids were raised. We wanted to share Dad's journey with friends and coworkers who can relate to, you know, what Dad went through with his health, and be an influence on them."

"I'm pleased that you had that desire," Mom said.

"There's actually more than that. Young and buzzing with excitement about our new love of each other, Dana and I were simultaneously witnesses to you and Dad and the whole ordeal. So, without anyone noticing, we recorded and documented the details of everything that happened with you and Dad, and turned it all into a book. In other words, you've been novelized, Mom!"

"My goodness!" she said, suddenly looking both happy and wistful, as if now she, too, was now yearning to remember it all, to let it flood back in. She appeared on the edge of something reawakening.

There was no turning back. This book had to get out. "Want to read it, Mom?" I asked, already standing up to walk across the room to my home office.

I opened a cabinet door and pulled out a blue binder with golden engravings, inside of which we had bound the sole existing printout of this book. Only recently, at long last and after scores of hours of labor, had Dana and I fleshed out the whole story.

I placed the binder on the coffee table in front of Mom.

"Take all the time you want, Mom," I said.

"A little chai, please, if you wouldn't mind, son. I'm going to be here for a while."

With a wrinkled left forefinger and thumb, Mom gently opened the first page and tilted her nurturing eyes down to read.

Section 1:

The Journey Begins

1

"I 'll be back in twenty minutes," said Gene Curtin. "I need some new nails to finish redoing your closet. I'll also hang the mirror on your closet door," he promised as he kissed his wife affectionately and strode out the door into the humid but slightly cool air.

"Gene..." Hope called after him, with an appreciative glance his way. "Drive carefully. I am making you dinner tonight, one of your favorites." Gene gave her a silent look of love that hadn't changed in twenty-nine years of marriage, and turned away. As Hope heard the powerful engine turn over in Gene's restored Chevy, she smiled inside.

On the drive to nearby Main Street Hardware, Gene was thinking about whether he'd be able to return home with all the parts, finish the job, and be ready for dinner, all the while imagining what that dinner would be.

Pulling into the small corner parking lot near the end of Main Street, he found a spot near enough the front door for his bones to manage. The old engine rumbled off as he removed the key from the ignition. After shutting the Chevy's clunky metal driver's-side door, the gait he used wasn't pretty, but it worked well enough today. A semisweaty moment later, Gene pulled open the swinging glass door to the air-conditioned store as the attached little bell clanged. As Gene said howdy to the familiar clerk, Charles, he made his way over to aisle 4.

With a bit of eyestrain, Gene held the box of nails up in front of his nose to examine them for the proper length and diameter. Through the blurriness, he made out that the box read "3.25 inch." As he took a step toward the counter, nails in one hand, his persistently achy ankle flared up, pain shooting through his knee and up to his hip and side. In the semibusy hardware store, forced to stop and gather himself in the aisle, Gene played it off as if he were looking at the boxes of screws on the next shelf over. Then he tried to walk again, this time shifting his weight gently more toward his toes, which caused the pain to feel less sharp as he walked. Keeping his weight on his toes seemed to offer a cushioning sensation. Gene let the memory of his lower body's agitation fade as quickly as it had arisen.

"How's it going, Gene? Another house project?" asked the owner of Main Street Hardware, who was acting as the clerk.

"It's my first love, Charlie," Gene replied, dressed in a sweatshirt bearing the logo of his son's Little League squad from a decade ago. "Hope's just so happy about our new house. Gosh, has it been four months in the place already? We're just getting to the closet! It's amazing she's so patient. I'm looking forward to getting this done. Thanks for all you've done for us."

"Happy to be able to help you, Gene. Now, take care of yourself as well as you do the house and Hope."

Gene emerged into the bright and hazy sunshine, as the shop door closed behind him with the jingle of bells. Gene's Corvair was only a few parking stalls away, mercifully. Charlie's comment echoed faintly in his ears. *Did he see pain in my face?* Gene wondered. *I'd be embarrassed if he did. At the same time, if he did, it is good that someone in this community cares enough to say something.*

The left turn out of the small parking lot onto Main Street led to a routine route home that allowed Gene to go into automatic pilot mode as he let his mind wander. He would use the medium-weight hammer to allow him control, leverage, and speed, so he could finish the closet and mirror jobs in time to sit at the table with his beloved Hope.

The next moment, Gene's left hand stopped picking up the sensation of the leather of the steering wheel. It was as though he simply had his hand out in front of him in empty space for no reason he could remember, as though he were sleepwalking. His right foot became disoriented and misinterpreted his brain's signals distinguishing the gas pedal from the brake. His eyes lost focus; was the weather hazier than he'd ever seen before? Everything around him began to dissolve; the car's dashboard first, followed by the rearview mirror, the car's hood, the dashed lane lines painted on the pavement, the island separating eastbound from westbound traffic, the traffic signs, and then the horizon itself deteriorated into gray, then bright light, then black.

Gene's consciousness wasn't even around for the crash.

2

"**W**ill he be OK?" Hope shrieked. Then she whimpered, "Mini-stroke, diabetic coma? I didn't even know he had diabetes."

The beeping of a hospital EKG ticked like a clock inside Hope's mind, counting the moments until unwelcomed news. She was remembering her and Gene's life together, the love for their child, the golden tinge their lives were beginning to take on despite all the challenges they had overcome. Seconds turned into minutes, minutes into hours, hours into tortured nights and days she moved through like a zombie.

—⟋⟍—

Gene and Hope were so much looking forward to their retirement. It would be the start of a new way of living, something they hadn't experienced in a long, long time. Gene had worked as an electrician, with almost equally good carpentry skills, for his whole life. From his early career as a solo contractor, kneeling on worn kneepads for full days plus overtime, he would complete his career as the president of a thirty-employee company. His was the firm that turned the lights on in many of the big, shiny buildings that were being built downtown. While everyone had watched the area modernize, Gene's electrical "empire" had networked the buildings with wire that carried the juice to run the glassy corporate fortresses. This brought Gene pride and as good a living as could ever have been imagined for an "electricianpreneur," as he liked to call himself.

Back before the rush to build in the very place where manicured riverfront properties now stood, Hope remembered studying swans that would spend precious weeks drinking and feeding along the banks of wild streams before continuing their migration across the plains and sloping valleys. She had been drawn to wildlife biology because she knew she was graceful like the wild birds. She also knew that her love was powerful, like a bear's. And like the great forests, she was fulfilled as long as she was providing a home for and nourishing others who were teeming with life and growth.

Hope had a saying about what happened for her when she met Gene during her first year as a biologist for the Department of the Interior. "I recognized you," she would say to Gene. She was using the biological jargon for the word "recognize." In wildlife biology, recognition is the moment a wildlife observer realizes what species he or she is looking at. Hope admitted that at one distinct moment, she had "recognition" of the "species" named Gene, and it was spelled M-Y F-U-T-U-R-E. Yes, she knew he would be very significant in her personal future.

In Hope's eyes, Gene embodied the arrow of time, inevitably leading toward the future, whether a fearsome future or one that provided comfort and brought fulfillment. When Hope glimpsed Gene in his work mode, she noticed a pattern in which he saw, spoke about, and created possibilities in whatever interaction he was having with a building client. The possibilities Gene saw for himself and his business in the future were also—and she loved this about him—possibilities for what their future as a couple could be.

In these forward-driven qualities of Gene, Hope found her contrast with her husband. Their differences happened to also drive a lot of their synergy. Hope could peer into the timeless elegance of a white swan's arching in shallow water at the stream bank and appreciate as a wildlife biologist how countless generations over eons have ingrained that unwavering behavior into the swan today. Left to just

7

be, it seemed that swan's behavior—and so much of nature—would continue on that way, timelessly. Hope was challenged, then, by modernization. Amid rapid technological development and growth, she felt as cornered as a trapped animal. Hope found so much balance in Gene because, instead of getting caught in powerlessness, he created ways to make the most out of modernization for the both of them.

Their retirement house was higher on St. Charles Hill than the house at the outskirts of downtown that they had lived in for the previous two decades. Up there, wild grasses still waved in the wind between well-spaced homes and subdivisions. Deer sometimes pranced there; neither a fox nor a coyote pack was a rare sight, and once in a while a wild swan would swoop in and drink from the dripping hose, the bird feeder, or one of the rechanneled drainage ditches between houses or running alongside driveways. Gene and Hope would be very whole and complete in this home for the rest of their days.

—⁓—

Early in their marriage, natural passions often gripped Hope and Gene. They were the meeting of growth and changelessness. They were an alchemy of the possibility that could be—and the drive to get there—matched with the observant quality of truly noticing what is now and what has always been. They raised their son with these two elements shaping his character. Sometimes they found it nerve-wracking, but they rested as easily as they could knowing that their son had flown the coop, and was making the transition into forging his own path, testing and retesting his own limits, and self-adjusting his own tendencies.

Retirement was to be, for Gene and Hope, the victory lap in a relationship that had taken them for an exhilarating ride quite a few times around the track. They counted their blessings that they had been able to live together and grow closer to each other while enjoying life in their quaint yet modernizing community, where they had both lived since they were children.

3

Gene's unconscious body had been found in an awkward position amid a tangle of steel that pressed upon him, limiting his blood's circulation. During his bedridden days, when Gene could neither make so much as an adjustment in his position nor give a report as to his sensations, no one from the outside, not even his doctors and nurses, could really know for sure what parts of his body may or may not have been receiving a sufficient stream of oxygenated blood.

The fact that Gene was, at least, breathing, provided Hope some comfort. She had not yet lost her husband. Their college-student son, Jim, had rushed there from his school across the state border, arriving by the morning after the accident and scarcely leaving Gene's bedside since then. Hope's still-doting mother, Sylvie, knitting as always, sat next to Hope, her usually nimble fingers trembling with concern.

Without Gene's subjective experience to inform them, the hospital team could only rely on their visual detection of skin coloring and discoloration to tell whether blood was reaching all of Gene's body parts. It happened on the third day of hospitalization and feeding tubes, with Gene still deep in a coma: significant discoloration of a patch of skin appeared on his right big toe and second toe.

"Administer antibiotics, and they'd better work quickly," said Dr. Fram, the lead unit surgeon. "While you're monitoring him, prepare a team for emergency amputation. We're not taking chances with this one."

It was four in the afternoon, and Hope was sitting with Sylvie in the Dignitea Tea Shop after spending all morning in the hospital yet again. Sylvie had always been a willing confidante for Hope, who now had more questions than she could really process. Her mother's caring ear was essential medicine for her.

They sat in silence by the window, a gloom over their table, amid sniffles and beads of tears in the corners of Hope's eyes. "Oh, God, Mom! I feel so bad for leaving the hospital," she said. "But I needed to be in a different space to process all of what's happening. Thanks for coming with me. Why is this happening, Mom?"

Sylvie stroked Hope's hand, having no words of comfort to offer. Yet even the soothing touch offered by her mother did not stop Hope's heart from jumping when her phone rang and she recognized the caller ID.

"Yes, this is Hope," she said into the phone.

"Hours ago, antibiotics were administered to combat the gangrene on Mr. Curtin's right toes," said the voice of the ward administrator. "Unfortunately, the response has not been favorable. The death of flesh is now seen in the tendon and connective tissue proximal to the toes. Dr. Fram has called for surgery immediately on Mr. Curtin's right foot, to amputate it below the metatarsals."

"Oh, God! I'll be there right away!" cried Hope, spilling some hot tea as she stood abruptly.

All Hope could see in her horrified mind was the surgical saw spinning at 5,000 rpm, even as she accelerated her minivan to the same revolutions while weaving through traffic.

"Call St. Joe's back, Mom," Hope said to Sylvie, who was sitting in the passenger seat. "We've got to talk to them before they start."

Sylvie pressed redial and managed to get through to the right extension. "Please put Dr. Fram on the phone," she said.

Sylvie addressed the surgeon with both pain and hope evident in her voice, "Dr. Fram, my son-in-law, Gene Curtin, has been in your hospital for three days, since almost immediately after his accident…

You haven't been able to prevent gangrene, and yet now we are expecting him to lose a foot because…"

Halting Sylvie, Dr. Fram interrupted, "Unfortunately, your son-in-law is in urgent need of a preventive amputation procedure in order to save his life and to stop the gangrene from spreading into his legs. Surgery is the best known preventive, and I have advised that the procedure take place at this time."

Hope pulled over and grabbed the phone from Sylvie. "But wait! There must be other treatments…" She was bawling, thinking about Gene's love of his independence, his home improvement projects, his car repair projects, his walks.

"Unless you choose to enforce your power of attorney and remove Mr. Curtin from this unit—at great risk to his life—the procedure on this patient will proceed, Mrs. Curtin," the doctor said.

Emitting a trembling, "Oh, please, God," Hope ended the call with Dr. Fram.

—◊—

A light appeared. Then it resolved into a light fixture embedded in the ceiling. Gene felt like he was waking up from the longest night of sleep he had ever had.

He sent his gaze a little lower and saw the differences in his feet at the end of the bed.

He remembered the foot problems he'd been having for longer than anyone knew, and Charlie's warning, "Take care of yourself," replayed in his mind. Then Gene remembered driving on Main Street…and then there was no more memory.

"Somehow, the surgical anesthesia—when it wore off, you woke up out of your coma," said Hope affectionately from his bedside. "Welcome back, honey."

"Yeah, welcome back, Dad!" Jim added.

"What's with my right toes?"

"They've assured all of us," Hope said with a gentle stroke of Gene's hand, holding back a salty tear, "that with a prosthetic, you should still be able to walk."

A silence ensued that in other circumstances would have been awkward. However, for Gene's family, after waiting for days while he was in a coma, a few more minutes of silence while he grew extremely pensive seemed, somehow, normal. Gene was gradually putting the pieces together about his life over the past…who knew how long. He occasionally grunted an *Aha*-like sound or changed his facial expression as what had happened began to click in his mind.

Gene realized that for some months now, he had been increasingly obsessive when thinking about water and food, with a sort of lust to get to the next meal (the last one being the dinner with his wife that had never happened). He had begun to lose feeling in his extremities—his toes and fingers. That was why he had felt less pain when walking with more weight on his toes and also why the first thing to disappear while driving before the accident was his sensation of the pedals and steering wheel. He also recalled how he had increasingly strained to read the print on boxes of tools. These were all, it turned out after a curt institutional briefing by a hospital staff worker, symptoms of type 2 diabetes.

He'd ignored and forced his way through all of it. Finally, when his system "crashed" (that's all he knew how to call it, and it was his pun on his car accident), everything he'd been ignoring seemed to attack him at the same time.

Gene felt sad for what he'd put Hope, Jim, and Sylvie through, angry that this was his fate, and intimidated at the odds that lay before him.

Yet he was still Gene. He never gave up on finishing projects. Dealing with diabetes would be another project to start, to work on, and, sometimes, to get around to.

"About that prosthetic foot. I'll be wanting to try that right away. There's still a mirror to install, if I remember," Gene said and smiled at Hope.

4

The diabetic protocol began in earnest when Gene first arrived home and unpacked the daily pillbox he'd gotten from the pharmacy. It was as organized as the nuts and bolts in a toolbox, so it was Gene's natural inclination to like following the routine, at first. He didn't quite like it as much by the second day, when he felt a little nauseated looking at the shiny, blue-gray chemical biotechnology products in his palm that were now his daily companions.

"Uh, I'm gonna test out these legs," he said, shuffling halfway to the front door.

"Let me come with you, just in case," Hope replied.

"Naw, honey, I'll be just on our block—back in five, ten minutes."

Ah, concrete beneath my shoes—that's more like it, he thought, standing on the top step as he left the house. *I've been rolled around on a bed or a wheelchair on linoleum floors, or helped to shuffle through my house on short carpet, for way too long. A man's soles have gotta touch hard rock every now and again.* He tried out a short step with his left leg and then a step with his right leg.

This is doable! he thought. *Today, I am going to get to that bush there, three doors down, and back, with as close to normal-looking strides as possible.*

—⁓—

"My grandson's baseball, lost for days," said a man who backed out, crawling, from under the thick bush just as Gene got there. "Hi, I'm Don," the man said, fingering the stitched seams of the ball in his left hand, extending his right hand to shake.

"Whoa, didn't expect you there, Don, is it?" said Gene in surprise. "But I guess that's what lost means—something not where you'd expect it."

"Couldn't have said it better myself, sir," Don agreed. "You look like you know this place well."

"Four months in the neighborhood, ten years in the town. Never saw a baseball hit on this street, though."

"We moved in Tuesday; didn't you see the truck? Couldn't miss that leviathan, I bet."

"Hmm, I was…not here."

Something moved in Gene as he realized that compared to hiding a grimace, hiding what he'd been through would be extremely difficult. This fellow, Don—Gene didn't know him at all, which meant he had no past with him. It somehow felt safe, meeting this new person who lived nearby but seemed, at least in Gene's assumptions, to have no association with the other connections in his life. Maybe this was a guy with whom Gene could loosen his burden, someone to come out to about what had happened.

"Didn't see it? Took a week off, eh?" asked Don.

"Um, kind of…I actually went into, um…I was, I had an acc…"

His thoughts raced; he found that he was uncomfortable talking about what had happened. He contemplated asking Don to come into his home, sit and talk, and meet Hope, but nervousness spoke in his mind. He was aware that Don hadn't seen him walking yet, and the effortful steps to get back home might give away something he wasn't quite ready to share.

On the other hand, now was the moment—to talk about where he was physically and mentally, or to stuff what was really going on with him back inside.

"You've just found a lost baseball, Don, but this week I lost something that's a part of me, which I can't ever get back," Gene said.

"Walk a few paces that way, Don," he continued, waving in the direction of his house. "But hand me the ball. I'll toss you a warm-up pitch, and if you catch it, we make a battery, catcher and pitcher. Then we'll talk.

"Oh, and whatever you do, don't let the ball bounce over into that driveway and ding up my pretty Chevy."

Don counted his steps methodically in the indicated direction, reaching the number ten—significantly less than half the distance from a regulation pitcher's mound to home plate, shy of even the Little League pitching distance.

"Perfect," Gene approved. "Now, I'm Tom Seaver pitching, and you're..."

"Gary Carter catching!" Don said, joining in the game.

"It's like the dead catching the living," Gene observed.

"We will see about that," Don said mysteriously.

Pitching involves standing on one foot and then planting your weight on the other foot. A mere strained toe has kept many a pitcher from his maximum performance. What Gene hoped to accomplish was a "toss," not a "pitch." All it would take was a sufficient transfer of energy from back to front, from the feet through the fingertips, to get the ball over to Don, on the mark.

For Gene's toss, what was left of his right foot and the prosthetic formed his foundation. Having any foundation down there at all felt precious now, where before he'd taken it for granted. Good Lord, he'd almost lost his foot! With a totally different sensation and new reality of support and trust in the body that he had left, he felt a surge of energy course from the earth into the baseball, with his body as a transfer medium.

"Stieeeeeeee-rrrrrrrriiiike!" Don exclaimed.

As with most ceremonial first pitches, the two walked toward each other. Gene didn't even notice whether Don perceived his odd strut.

As he displayed the caught baseball in the palm of his left hand, Don cheered Gene's physical ability, affirming, "Now that's a battery!"

—ɷ—

"I can't believe I'm telling you I have diabetes, which is news I just learned," Gene declared cathartically. "I've never been one to admit to my weaknesses or share my health condition; those have been things 'for me to know and for you to find out,'" he continued, noticing the irony of his own statement with a wince and a chuckle.

"You're lucky to be alive, Gene. But you're unlucky to have missed that dinner, though," Don joked.

"Tell me about it," Gene quipped, leading to a reflective pause.

After a moment, Gene said, "You know, Don, this is totally brand new to me, having the name of a disease to go with the way I'm feeling. It's like I bought the suit. Do you know what I mean? I'm not just trying it on anymore. It feels like I have to walk out of the fitting room, wearing it now and forever."

"I get what you mean by 'new,' Gene," Don said. "The progression of diabetes is really just beginning in you. You're at day one, or two, or whatever it is. You're in the infancy of the effect diabetes can have on your life."

Gene felt the sting of the possibility that Don might be right. Blunt...but right.

"I don't know, Don, I'm on the program—I promised myself and my wife that—so I think it'll be fine now. Now I know what I'm in, what game I'm playing. I wasn't even aware I was diabetic until now, and I think doing what they say now, it's like I know the rules of the game and I'll play it just fine."

Gene had to admit, though only to himself, that Don's warning was exactly what he'd been avoiding thinking about—avoiding it angrily, in fact. To bring up such a morose concern in front of Gene was to tempt his pent-up frustration.

Like a reflex, Gene's harsher side snapped into action and occupied his thoughts: *Maybe Don here on the corner is a little new himself to neighborly conversation. How could he say that to me, at a time like this?*

Don said, "Gene, I'm not saying that to scare you," as if reading Gene's mind.

Now Gene had a moment of regretting having opened up. The feelings of being vulnerable in his own body, afraid, ashamed—which he had transcended momentarily through baseball and bonding—rushed back in.

"Hey, Don, take care. I—I gotta head back in," Gene said.

He didn't even mention the late-afternoon glare now adding to the challenge of walking back home. Vision used to be no problem for him, but now that he admittedly struggled with it, he realized how much he missed having the vision he'd enjoyed in the past.

Gene turned on his right foot to face homeward, feeling his weight rest upon that new foundation below his ankle, part man and part medical machine. As he strode gingerly on his left foot and then on his right, Gene heard a slow whisper, either in the rustling leaves or from the mysterious neighbor two paces directly behind him:

"I didn't want to hear about it, either, Gene."

It was true: Gene really didn't want to hear another word of his weakness. Whoever it was who had said that—the wind, his own mind, or his "Jerk-el"-and-Hyde new neighbor Don, Gene just kept walking.

5

Hope was sleeping. She wore her graying hair in a cropped style above the shoulders, but the short locks betrayed a flowing quality which often moved Gene to pleasurably run his hands through its waves. Her arched nose, with its smallish nostrils, barely peeked from under the old cream-colored blankets into the semilit dawn of their master bedroom.

The rhythm of her breath continued uninterrupted as Gene maneuvered to plant his feet on the floor. His pajama-clad body sat on the edge of their bed. Below his knees the pajama pants came to an end, so Gene noticed his wide calves, which were always muscular yet had softened with age. He saw the familiar veins of his calf muscles punctuate the contours of his slightly sagging tanned skin.

After a pause, Gene eventually pulled his middleweight body out of bed.

The paper, it occurred to him. *That's what I want. A breakfast date with* The Townland Post.

Plodding in one flip-flop out to the driveway (he hadn't bothered trying to figure out how to slip his prosthetic into the right flip-flop), Gene's still-rigid strides were nevertheless growing more fluid as he gained confidence in balancing on his prosthesis. He appreciated the morning air.

Planting his weight on both his sandaled, natural left foot and his bare, prosthetic right foot, Gene bent down for the paper.

The newspaper was folded normally, bound by its usual eraser-red-colored rubber band. There was, however, on this particular morning, some kind of an insert tucked into the rubber band, which had the effect of blocking the front-page headline.

How annoying.

Still, Gene's gaze locked on to the face in the photo of a lone man bulging out of his clothes. His image lacked life; he had plenty of chins and looked as if he might close his eyes and pass out in the next moment. *Probably a new local real-estate agent or small-claims lawyer getting his forgettable face known to the community*, Gene thought.

Gene turned over the photo, printed on card stock paper, to see who this guy was.

In the place of where Gene expected an overdone advertisement and large, bolded phone number, instead were written in faded pencil, three lines, reading:

A1C: 10.1
Blood sugar: 262
Weight: 272

What? Gene thought, his heart skipping a beat and his mind racing at the mystery.

Then it hit him. At that moment, he knew whose plump, pocked, padded face it was in the old photograph.

"That rascal!"

6

"Hope, I don't know if this block is big enough for two diabetics. There is something so uneven about the way we talked to each other; I noticed it last night," Gene said.

"What do you mean, 'uneven'?" Hope asked.

"He goes ahead and talks about things I've got no intention on Earth of talking about…Well, maybe I'd say these things to you, or to a doctor—but probably not even to Jim. To Don, they were no big thing at all! I couldn't take all that talk about 'the infancy of diabetes' and its effect on my life. Who the hell wants to think about that stuff, let alone talk about it?"

"So you just don't want to talk about the future of what this new situation looks like, is that it, honey? At least not right now?"

"Absolutely, that's right."

There was a pregnant pause as Hope empathetically took in her husband's words. Finally, she said, "But I sure am curious, darling, 'cause that was an old photo…I am wondering what *his* experiences have been in all the years he's had diabetes. Aren't you curious?"

After a beat, she added, "I can't imagine what you're going through and I am only suggesting here, but maybe it would be good for you to let him know how you feel, Gene. Deep down, I sense you're wanting to know the things you'd rather not talk about. Besides," she let out a half laugh, "I'm curious what has happened with him between that photograph and now. I mean, from what you told me, he's been playing baseball with his grandson, slimming down, and— I'm inferring—looking more alert than he was in that old photo."

"OK, babe, OK," Gene said, both to dismiss the topic and soothe his wife. "Hey…what's for dinner?"

7

The humidity was just as heavy, if not more so, than the day that had changed Gene's life the previous week. This time, the breeze brought about a different feeling, however. Whereas most humid days seem to have only haze, today there were clearly visible thick, puffy clouds blowing by, contrasted against a deep blue sky.

"Mind if I climb your fence? My ball flew over it into your yard," huffed and hollered an out of breath boy as he rapped on the Curtins' front door.

Hope, hearing a cacophony that drew her toward her front door, past the coat hooks, calmly swung the door open. Gathering what the situation was about, she smiled at the boy's predicament and called, "Gene!" Her voice carried down the hallway into the garage where Gene was tinkering around. "I think you oughta come deal with this. It's about a baseball inside our fence around the side of the house. And a young man you'd like to meet," she added.

Getting to his feet anytime he was sitting at his work desk was now a chore, a skill that Gene had had to relearn now that it involved minutely different weight-bearing angles upon his foot and prosthesis. "Yaahhhppp. Agggh. Yep, coming."

Using his improved hobble, Gene took more than a minute to arrive at the entranceway. Beholding the little enthusiastic creature, Gene authoritatively invited him, "You can come around through the gate, but I'd like to know your name."

"I'm Nat," the boy said, tapping a size-four cleat against the ground as he started dashing to the gate to seek out the ball.

The ball was somewhere out of sight in the yard. Nat wasn't sure where it would have flown and bounced to, as the fence and vines were not easy to see through from the street. Under the bird feeder, behind the stacked-up shovels, even inside the drainpipe he looked and looked and looked. And looked some more, testing Gene's patience.

"I'm going to go back into the garage," Gene said to the eager boy. "You just keep looking. And please close the gate on your way out."

Since he really did have a lot on his mind, including how in the world he was going to get a grip psychologically, let alone physically, on his diabetes, Gene didn't feel quite himself, and he wasn't quite as personable with the lad as he might have been.

"Nat, are you in there?" came a call from the street side of the fence, just as Gene was walking away from the yard. Gene knew that voice was Don's. It was amazing how his face and his voice were ingrained so clearly in Gene's memory.

"Yeah, Grampa, I'm in the yard looking for the ball!" Nat shouted.

"What a surprise, Gene!" Don exclaimed when his and Gene's routes crossed at the open gate to the backyard.

"Hi there, Don," Gene said, feeling awkward and slightly rushed, having a scheduled medication to take. "Uh, yeah, your grandson knocked it over the fence so good that he's still looking for it. I gotta…"

"Hah, nice one," Don chimed in appreciation of their continuing baseball-influenced communication. "So what's going on?"

Opting to answer that quickly, strictly in terms of a lost leather ball and getting Don to take responsibility for removing Nat from his backyard, rather than reveal any information about himself from the past few days, Gene said, "Your grandson—nice kid, by the way—is searching the back and side yards again and again for a ball he is sure flew in here."

"Hey, Nat…" Don called him over. "So, whatcha doing?"

"I'm looking for the baseball."

"Are you sure it's along the side of the backyard?"

"Um, no. I thought it actually just flew in here by a little."

"So why are you looking all the way down the side into the back?"

"Because I can see back there. I am looking wherever I can see."

"Where do you really think it is?"

"It would be closer to the front, near here."

Just then, the three of them all had their eyes drawn to the leaves and lawnmower clippings piled up in the front corner of the yard, shaded in the darkness of the corner by the thick vines that overhung the fence.

Nat was now in *there*, up to his elbows and knees, before anything else could be said. The pile was probably the least visible place to find a ball that the yard had to offer. But it wasn't twenty seconds before Nat had found it.

"Couldn't see it, but I found it!" he gleefully screeched.

"You are going to rake the pile back up, right, Nat?" Don instructed. "I'll let you use our rake."

"OK, Grampa. But if I could use the one in the backyard, that would be faster. I know exactly where it is. It's in the back."

"I'm sure you do," said Don and Gene simultaneously, chuckling.

"Sometimes we just look where we can see, right, Gene?" Don asked.

What? Gene thought.

Don turned his attention to Nat, and said, "Go back on home; you've been out a long time. Tell Gramma I'm at our neighbor Gene's for a few minutes."

—⁓—

"It's hard to see the ball if it's buried in clippings and hidden from the light," Don mused.

Not certain of Don's point, Gene joined in anyway: "...when the well-lit and freshly mowed yard makes for such an easy place to keep looking."

"Yes, sir, you've got it," Don said encouragingly.

"I got what?" Gene asked, puzzled. "I know Nat finally got his baseball, when he dropped his bias in favor of looking where the light and terrain makes everything easier to see."

"Yes."

"Um, listen, Don. This isn't how I normally get to know someone. I missed your move-in by being hospitalized, I feel traumatized in the gut by the time I'm done talking with you, I find your picture and medical statistics in my morning paper when I just wanted to sit down for breakfast and read the news, and now I have the distinct feeling I am getting underhandedly lectured, in parable, about a boy finding his lost baseball. It's like I've lost one of my feet and now am feeling half-mad, except everything mad that is happening between us, whoever you are, is kind of real, too."

Gene got choked up at that moment, a sob lodged in his larynx. "Too real, maybe. And that could be the thing that I'm not used to about this…this change in my life."

Don pulled his sweatshirt up from his waist to his belly, revealing a tattoo that read simply, *Get Real.* "This is the exact spot where I used to inject the insulin into my body," he revealed.

"Whoa," came out of Gene's lips. He knew that "whoa," in this case, actually matched what he was really feeling deep inside. "Um, Don, so the you standing here in front of me and the you in that photograph look completely different," he said, searching for an explanation.

"It was *where I looked.* It was my choice where to look, as it is your choice where to look, as it is young Nat's choice where to look. Think about that."

"That's easy to think about. I don't get it, and I know I don't get it. That's all the thought I have on that, Don."

Don asked, "Where was Nat looking first?"

"Along the side, toward the backyard."

"And why?"

"Because he could see there." Gene tired of the questions.

"True, true. Now answer for yourself: Where are you looking?" Don looked directly at Gene.

"I'm looking at...I'm looking at...How did you go from that photo and your obvious signs of serious illness, like insulin injections, to where you are now? And I'm looking at my son, Jim, and my wife, Hope."

"Keep going."

"I'm looking at being told about these blue pills and that I should have only so many starchy pastries, sausage only a few times per week..."

"And?"

"I'm looking at just hoping that'll keep me from going blind, or losing more limbs or organs, Don! They say the treatment will at least delay and maybe stop those things from happening."

"Have you told me all you see?" Don asked earnestly.

"I guess so..." Gene trailed off.

Don then squared his shoulders with Gene's and said, "People looking for something have two options: they can either look until they find it, or they can give up before they find it."

He continued, "You can pretty well tell which choice I made. Your choice is up to you."

"There's a lot there, Don," Gene replied. "Usually, up until now, when I've had a choice, I've known the options."

"Exactly, Gene!" Don said. "That's the whole baseball-in-the-leaf-pile thing. When you only look where it's most brightly lit, what are you risking?"

"Never finding the ball, I suppose," Gene said, catching on further.

"Good. So how do you mitigate that risk?"

"Like Nat did eventually?" Gene offered.

"You're on the right track!"

Gene said, "What I saw Nat do is finally look where it wasn't necessarily so easy to see."

"Bingo."

"So I would say Nat 'dug in.' Are you telling me the key is digging in, Don?"

"I pretty much am, Gene," Don replied.

"Great," Gene exhaled, "'cause the way Hope cooks, I look forward to my 'dig in' time every day—right around this time!—so I really gotta go."

"Ha," Don laughed, almost brotherly. "Gene, I like your sense of humor."

"*Catch* you later," quipped the guys to each other at the same time, the fun of their conversation peaking.

What prevailed in that moment was their common humanity and their discovery that, even in their different current states of health, they now shared a context. Both men stirred with new viewpoints and possibilities and a bit of fire within their bellies (of several kinds). Don maneuvered out through the fence, heading home to his awaiting grandson. Meanwhile, Gene, a notch more confidently, strode up the steps into his savory-smelling kitchen, the hearth of his home.

8

Hope and Gene both found themselves swooping down on the dinner table, as best they could given their respective physical conditions, enlivened by their expectant taste buds and lovers' hearts. Gene was just coming in, and Hope, who had been cooking for some time, was just venturing out of the kitchen when they nearly bumped into each other in the kitchen doorway.

In that moment of warm physical proximity, Hope said, "Gene, I love you so much, and I want to talk with you." She and Gene both made their hungry descent upon the table and landed in their chairs.

"What about?"

"I want to do what's best for you. Have you been in touch with anyone who's able to share some eating tips for people with diabetes?"

This was the first time it had really been brought to their consciousness that they had been avoiding that question, less out of evasion and more out of cluelessness in terms of where to start.

"Hmm, how to eat, eh?" Gene said, more acknowledging the question than answering it. "Let's do some eating, and let our, er, our mouths do the talking," he said as both he and Hope broke into laughter at the awkwardness of the double function of "mouths" creating a failed pun. Laughter had always been a most powerful icebreaker in their partnership, warming them up in many ways.

"He-e hee! I've always liked your mouth, Gene," Hope, flirting with her long-time partner. "Look at this, just imagine it: through your diabetes, we have been given an opportunity to learn all kinds of new ways that we can use our mouths together. I kinda like the sound of that."

"Hope, you always make it such a pleasure to be alive, no matter what's going on," Gene said romantically.

"Hey, food is sexy," she said. "Classical Roman poets all the way through modern psychological studies concur. The *Kama Sutra*, Hollywood movies, the Biblical psalms, those fond of nature worship…from what I've come across in my life, all of them converge on the conclusion that food is the way to sass each other up!"

"Magazines," Gene contributed, "also magazines. I mean, how many popular magazines, like the ones you see at the market, put out issue after issue filled with articles on people's sex lives *and* on making delicious food? 'Coincidences' like that don't last thirty years. There's something there."

"Sweetheart, look no further than right here. There's no time I feel more attracted to you than after being provided for with a good, vital meal by someone I love…you!

"In fact, we conceived Jim on a rainy afternoon just like that. You'd ordered in from my absolute favorite place—let's see if you remember what it was—for a Saturday afternoon of…how did I describe it to my girlfriends? Oh, yes: a scrumptious snuggling Saturday!"

"Wow, weren't those the days? Would food turn us on now the way it did back then?" snorted Gene cynically.

"Gene, listen to me. Those were *those* days. *Of course* things have changed…biologically. You know, from university biology onward through my Fish and Wildlife career, we carefully studied the cycles in which everything ages and dies, going back into the soil."

Gene said softly, "Yeah, I know, Hope, the natural cycle—you see life through that."

"But I think I told you about this before," Hope continued. "As I got older, I had lots of freedom to reflect on my academic career. As much as we biologists see patterns in the wild that reflect the theories in our textbooks, something was missing. I didn't have to overly superimpose the concepts from textbooks onto my personal life, Gene...our life, you and me. In fact, it didn't work out so well at all when I tried to shape our life from textbook theories, Gene."

Now Gene was intrigued, by the sex part as well as by the fact that his wife was exposing to him something new that was going on with her.

In a soft, attentive voice, he said, "Please, continue. I was with you up until the 'superimposing' part."

"I'm just seeing that you and I are having a subjective experience I'll never—no wildlife biologist will ever—be able to record in nature, because it *is* subjective! At that point, biological theories become something we brush up on in order to understand the small part of reality that our careers will depend on. It's not the total truth to see our own life transitions only through the observable biological lens. The theories are meant to bend and change as we observe new things in nature. Today's textbooks aren't like yesterday's, and tomorrow's will be different from today's. There's never been another Gene Curtin, and there's never been another Hope Curtin."

Eyes gleaming, Hope inclined her head toward Gene across the dinner table. "It's got me so inspired, Gene. We can't be certain what will happen. We don't have one set theory to predict what's going to become of us, either one of us, Gene."

It was a side of Hope that was visible rarely enough for it to be special, when her observant nature made a breakthrough in perception. At those points, when she felt comfortable and paid attention to by Gene, she would lay out her new discovery or finding.

These moments throughout their marriage had led to Gene's peaks of closeness with his wife. Whereas he was the one driving forward, creating pragmatic possibilities for their future, every once in a while, Hope's quiet side would erupt into realizing something great and broad about the universe and human beings' context within it. There, they met: she in moving her deep, wide-eyed experience of life a quantum leap forward, and he, for once in a blue moon, dropping his incessant drive to produce progress in his business and being overcome with an awe for the profound, as embodied and expressed by Hope.

"So what I'm saying, Gene, is we're conscious and we're alive. Sure, we have slower impulses and more saggy skin. What I say is, as long as we're breathing, there is plenty of uncertainty that what I called scrumptious snuggling Saturday is alive and well. Heck, we're retired! What does Saturday have to do with it anymore? I'm already turned on—in my heart, Gene—to create food for us to eat that will turn us on to the fact that we are alive and conscious, that we can share together. And who knows what will happen when we do that?

"Find out, Gene…Find out how to eat for where you are in your life right now."

"Hmm. How, indeed?" Gene mused. "I will—I will find out, I promise. For now, I know it's time to dig in. Let's dig in together, Hope, it's dinnertime."

9

What on Earth, Gene pondered, *do I do? Where do I start? How do I eat for having diabetes? And for wanting to be there with Hope all the way through our lives and wanting to see Jim grow up and have a family of his own?*

After dinner with Hope, these were the thoughts that Gene had gone to sleep with.

In the morning, after a clear sunup, as Hope woke up and boiled some water for tea, she could hear Gene speaking, apparently into the phone, from the living room: "I nearly died, Dr. Fram, and that's why I'm calling you. Being in a wreck and having to be taken to the ER in an ambulance, unconscious, is a situation I'd like to…you know… avoid in the future. What can I do to be most assured to prevent that? To get, yeah, to get physically to where that could not happen again?"

"Good question," Hope whispered to her morning tea.

"Oh, uh-huh. OK, I see. Yeah, gosh, aging tissues, yeah, that's sure true!…Yeah, um, OK, Doc, uh, thanks again. I'll let you go, because I can tell you have another person to save, just like you did for me. Yep, ummm, g'bye."

Gene got off the phone. Feeling satisfied, he took a step by bearing down on his prosthesis, feeling what rocking from heel to toe on fiberglass was like. Next, he set his opposite foot, his remaining biological foot, onto the floor and felt what its rocking action was like. Then, once again, his prosthesis found the floor. This repetition of steps allowed him to gravitate toward the kitchen, where Hope sat at the table, soaking a tea bag in her mug.

"Highest-paid doc in the county just gave me the answer, Hope! I'm aging along with my tissues. Diabetic complications are gonna

31

happen again, maybe any day. We just try to delay it and keep the other problems from getting really bad by controlling carb and sugar levels with my pills at the ready for when I feel that woozy feeling again. That's it, that's what he said. Sounds like a pretty clear and scientific final answer to me."

Hope was blowing a light stream of air into her tea, and as she heard what Gene was relating to her about his conversation with Dr. Fram, he noticed her purse her lips.

Scientific? she thought. *What science was being applied in that conversation to how the body worked?* Speaking aloud, Hope prompted her husband, "Gene, remember the walnut trees you once helped me transplant along Riverbank Park as part of our watershed wildlife restoration?"

"I sure do. Dang, it almost wasn't worth it; the next two years, those trees didn't give a single walnut. The wildlife agency sued the orchard for selling sick trees, but fortunately for the orchard, they had the records to prove those trees had had twenty-three years of yielding good walnuts. What a laugh!"

"Do you remember what I told you that Professor Grepon, the botanist, said in his five-year report on the outcome of the transplant?" Hope asked, to test Gene.

"I think, by that point, the transplanted trees had produced marvelous walnut harvests for three years and counting. They inferred the two-year misfiring was from the poor soil that was initially in Riverbank before the new dirt got delivered. Oh, and the couple of drought years early in the decade could have killed the trees if they had tried to produce walnuts. The trees were holding back to conserve energy and water. Smart things, those trees."

"You really listened, Genie!"

"Well, I'm really glad the trees lived, because, you know, we get to power the lighting displays the city sets up around those tree trunks and branches during the holidays."

"Walking there with you in the winter is beautiful, honey," Hope said with a grin. "Now let me ask you: if, for just one minute, you could be a biologist, what would you notice about Professor Grepon's report—you know, the one that explains how we have the walnut trees thriving today?"

"Well, bad soil and rainless springs sent the trees to shit for a spell there. Then...whoa!" Rocking back, at that moment Gene had a revelation. "When you think about it this way, I mean, like I said, that period could have killed them. But they pulled in their seeds for a while, rode out the storm, if you will, and then, sure enough, *dug in* until some better soil and water came along for their roots."

Hope asked, "Are you thinking what I'm thinking? Gene, I swear, this morning when I got out of bed, I did not realize those trees were going to teach us something that could massively change our lives, but now, I do believe we're starting to get a picture—and we're getting it together!"

"Hope, if you, as a biologist, were going to say what walnut trees 'eat,' would you say..."

"Soil nutrients and water."

"I knew it. Nutrients. Water...I get it now, Hope!"

"Gene, you've always powered the lights, while I observed the power. Now I think we're both seeing the light."

"Hardy har har, little lady! You might say the light is 'planted' in my brain!"

—⟋⟋⟋—

The rest of the morning seemed to carry them along in a dance. They suddenly felt the despairing tone of recent times soften its grip and give way to the unmistakable sense of potential in the air. The last time they'd felt this inspired was actually before the accident itself. It went back to the feeling they'd had more than five years before when they envisioned the home they would move to after a well-timed retirement. They had pictured the way the light would reflect off the hills into their living room window about an hour before sunset. They had pictured a home that would enable Jim see what success after a well-lived life could look and feel like.

They had known a new life was waiting for them up on this hill. They were expecting a change of address and a change of vantage point. Little did they know that moving to this space would be the harbinger of much, much more change.

The Internet at the Curtin home suddenly became a download machine for nutrition articles, fitting for a scientist at work. Hope also opened up the kitchen cupboard doors and left them that way— for better viewing makes for better scrutiny and pondering. As a third line of attacking the home's nutrition challenge, Hope decided to call up her son to enlist his help.

"Jim…Good, I'm glad you're enjoying class. Study up for that midterm," Hope began, excited to get to the topic at hand. "Now, Jim, I have a request for you. Your father and I are going to study. Yes, I know it sounds funny. We'd really appreciate it if you saved us the trip over there to State U. Would you take out some books from the university's library for me? I know you're in the middle of studying and, of course, you're busy with your friends, but do you have time this weekend to bring the books over to us? You do? Oh, Jim, I really appreciate this, and I'll explain why later. Would you please just get anything having to do with nutrition, aging, or diabetes, OK? Great, Jim, thanks. I love you. See you and a load of literature this weekend."

10

The living room was covered with journals and books sprawled all over the place like a chaotic family library. Gene, Hope, and Jim were all there, devouring numerous articles and book chapters. Enjoying the opportunity to be with his family on a special mission, Gene had struggled and eventually managed, on his still-uncertain footing, to carry his work chair from the converted garage workshop into the living room. It was all a sign of the unity and total enthusiasm for learning from humanity's most brilliant researchers on metabolism, physiology, and nutrition that had gripped the Curtin family as they focused on restoring the body's health. Total enthusiasm was seen—that is, except from Gene himself, who was caught in a form of reluctance, like inertia to his old ways, despite seeing, intellectually, how this research would be good for him.

Yet now, as the sun reached its zenith, Gene was ready for a break. He was also thrilled to be with his son, home from college, and expressed his love as teasing Jim about his studious nature. In a peppy and snarky tone, Gene said, "Well, that was fun."

Gene's tone of voice informed Jim that if his dad had truly finished his thought, he would have gone on to say, "…kinda the way geeks say starting a new class at school is 'fun.'"

Playfully retaliating for the ribbing his dad was giving him, Jim asked, "Done already, Dad?" joshing his old man about his stamina. That play wasn't new. He'd done it since he was a preteen, when he'd subtly picked up on the gradual decline of his father's physical edge.

Suddenly, their banter was interrupted by Hope's emerging from the hall closet with her long-stored-away twenty-four-inch flip chart.

"We're going to publish our main discoveries from the literature here on this poster paper, everyone!" Hope announced with the pride of a scientific congress moderator. "Main ideas on the first page and then each subsequent page for details on each of the main ideas."

Amazed at the way Hope was organizing this project and keeping it moving forward even when he was ready for a break, Gene sat there with his mouth slightly agape until Jim shook him out of it with a whispered, "Uh, Dad, you're drooling…Gotcha!"

Hope, ringing the metaphorical school bell, which caused the two men in the house to respond very differently, asked like a team leader, "Who's going first? What is the main point of the articles they read?"

While Gene's impulse was to escape to his workshop and tinker—an urge held at bay only by the stacks of books and papers in the room—Jim eagerly walked up to the flip board. Hope handed him a thick permanent marker with which to compose the first subject title. Just as Jim opened his mouth to deliver an oration of his discovery to his parents, the doorbell rang.

Young, limber, and easily switching between things, Jim adjourned his presentation, high-stepped over the open books, and said just as he got to the door, "Don't worry, I'll get it!"

As Jim opened the door and more daylight streamed into the Curtin home, a cheery voice emerged from a bright-eyed, warmly smiling woman standing on the porch. She had a petite, attractive figure and appeared older than middle-aged. She sported a vibrant aura and a clear, olive complexion. She was wearing a green-and-white, pearlescent-hued necklace. The matching earrings she wore had a distinctive pattern of greenish pearlescent stones, which Jim noticed. He thought for a moment—abstract college thinker that he was—that the layout of the earrings appeared to portray a sun with seven planets.

"Hi, I'm Rima, Nat's grandma and Don's wife," the woman said. "And who do I have the pleasure of meeting?"

"Jim, back for the weekend from college. You must know my parents. Who are Nat and Don?"

Gene and Hope could hear this exchange taking place at the door and could hardly help but notice the synchronicity of their big day of discovery and Rima's decision to come by. They looked at each other: from the confidence of her introduction, they could tell that Rima packed at least the mysterious wallop that Don did and that this family nutrition study session was going to go beyond what they had expected or hoped.

"Yes, um, Rima, come in; it's just that our house is a little, um, disorganized right now," Gene called, elevating his voice so he could be heard from the living room, but hesitant about her seeing what he and his family were up to. "Thank you for coming by."

Gene wanted the physical capability to be able to meet Rima by leaping out of his seat and hopping over the stacks of books like Jim had done, but instead slightly cringed and waited as Jim led her on a meandering path through the front hall and the living room, where the books were piled up. Across a crate upon which sat one of the opened books, Rima and Gene extended their hands toward each other and shook as new acquaintances. Rima then extended an especially warm smile toward Hope, and the two women shook hands with friendly vim and vigor.

"How are Nat and Don?" Gene asked, feeling a semblance of a bond with them, which surprised him.

"Oh, great! Soaking up the sun's rays at the ball game together," Rima replied sweetly. "Kind of you to ask."

Rima, with palms open and her hands spread out to take in the scene inside the house, took in a deep breath that seemed to open her eyes a little wider and bring even more of a flush to her skin.

"Well!" She exhaled and paused.

"Yes, it's quite a day for us today, as you can see," Hope said breathily. "Since you're here, and I'm not sure about the purpose for your visit, how would you like to join our scientific presentation of what we as a family have been studying since last night and the break of dawn this morning?"

"What a lovely idea—count me in, Professor!" Rima exclaimed. This was received with some joy and a definite buildup of energy among the household.

"I believe I was about to present a main topic on nutrition," said Jim, who had already returned to the flip chart, pulling the marker out of the pocket of his slightly saggy pants. Meanwhile, Hope sat on the couch facing the flip chart, Gene returned to his work chair, and the diminutive Rima stood behind and in between Hope and Gene.

Back in his imagined professor's lectern, Jim began, "The topic sentence is 'Research shows that the unit of health is the house-hold—it is easier for a family to shift its eating patterns and lifestyle than for an individual.' It is also harder for a community to shift its patterns than a household. Not too big, and not too small, a house-hold sharing a kitchen and table is the unit most effective at becoming healthier."

Jim completed his speaking time at the Curtin conference center "podium" by writing in blocky letters near the top of the flippable page:

THE UNIT OF HEALTH IS THE HOUSEHOLD.

The audience of three applauded wildly. Jim bowed to the ovation awkwardly, and with some obvious pride took his seat.

"Who is next?" Hope asked, half knowing it was either herself or Gene.

Gene got up, made sure he was standing solidly on his foot and prosthetic, and, with noticeably little cynicism, lumbered toward what was becoming their scientific poster. Hope and Jim, both proud, looked on. Rima, too, paid attention.

Gene began, "The main topic I discovered is, 'What we eat flips the switches that determine our health. If we learn the switches, we have a lot of power over our health.' As an electrician, when I discovered books and articles about food and the human body's epigenetic switches, something that had never happened before—outside of business and electrician training manuals—I couldn't stop reading. Through the power we have over what nutrition we give our body to deal with, our relationship to food is like the switchboard operator's relationship to the electricity in entire building complexes."

Completing his presentation with distinction, Gene composed the letters:

FOOD FLIPS THE SWITCHES OF OUR HEALTH.

Hope and Rima exchanged impressed glances. "Wow! Woo-hoo, sexy man!" Hope screamed, acting younger than her years and completely enthusiastic about Gene's biological discovery and that he'd combined this discovery with his area of expertise, making the information he had available into a practical source of personal power. She placed her palms on Gene's temples and planted two kisses on him, one on his forehead and one on his lips, as her eyes began to well, which brought a creased smile to his face.

Not one to let things get out of control while she was visiting, Rima cleared her throat. She said gently, yet with a certain anticipation of what the matriarch of the house would offer, "I suppose it is your turn now, Hope."

"Yes, well," Hope began, patting at the moistness in the corner of her eye with a tissue and clearing the frog from her throat. "What I want to start with is to say something important to me, that wildlife biology has been such a part of much of my life, and as my life work, it's been..."

Hope paused, this time wiping her right eye with her whole hand.

"But it is a whole different thing—oh, my gosh, let me tell you— to recognize my husband, my son, and myself as physically very similar in meaningful ways to the forests and wetlands I have 'adopted,'"

Hope said, faithfully returning to the theme of recognition, her favorite theme when expressing things to people she loved.

"I am standing here a biologist, an expert in the nutrient cycle—or what we call in big science talk the trophic cycle, because 'trophic' means energy. Yet here, in the last third of my life, I find myself having to pull an emergency all-weekend study jam with my family in order to pull my husband back from the brink of death from type 2 diabetes. God willing, after we help my husband resolve his healing saga well, we will have also helped my son not have to suffer difficulties like this one in his future."

Something occurred to Hope as she spoke. "Oh, amazing! I swear, if Jim were to get diabetes later in life—and I pray he does not—now that would have appeared to be evidence that type 2 diabetes runs in our family. But after hitting the books, even if Jim gets diabetes when he's older, I'd know eating and lifestyles both early and later in life caused it," she said. The scientist, the wife, and the mother spoke together for one of the first times in her life.

"Gene, and Jim, and yes, you, too, Rima: now I know what people mean when they call our scientific theories 'half-brained,' using our deductive-reasoning left brain and neglecting our practical sides. I hadn't given one-half of a thought to applying the nutrient cycle to our own family. Pin me to the wall, because today I am a perfect half-brained specimen!" effused Hope. "It hardly took a PhD for me to recognize, so long ago, that being planted in nourishing soil is what gives walnut trees and every other kind of tree access to the vital nutrient cycle. And the wild animals—bless their hearts as we demolish more and more habitat—still live in the wild and are able to eat as nature intended, without observed obesity, diabetes, overinflammation, heart disease, Alzheimer's, stroke..." she added poignantly.

Coming to her climactic main point, Hope shared with her family and Rima, "Yet up to this moment, I didn't recognize that we, too, are intended by nature to eat natural and wild foods. Only trees planted in quality natural soil have the ability to effectively metabolize, respire, grow, heal, and detoxify. Likewise, for us to grow, we need a balanced input of nutrition, as nature provides. What is true in my beloved ecosystems is as true in my most beloved people."

OUR INTESTINES ARE OUR ROOTS.

was the inscription Hope penned on the flip chart using the thick, navy blue marker.

After Hope's passionate lecture ended and she came down off the "podium," she leaned over to again plant a peck on her beloved Gene, this time on the lips. She then reached out for her son's hand and squeezed, with pride in her eyes.

Sensing the genuine power this family had through its love—not her family, but one she had been increasingly relating to—Rima sat on the edge of her seat. Her lit-up eyes and flushed cheeks betrayed that she was viewing something of immense intrigue for her. If she had been an opera aficionado, she would have worn the same expression if she had been in Italy's *Teatro alla Scala*.

Despite the slight awkwardness of the fact that Rima, a woman they had never met before, was present for their catharses of intellectual and emotional understanding of familial wellness, the Curtins had become, somehow, intuitively aware that in the craft of transforming the possible, Rima was an aficionado indeed, if not a maven and master. And they were about the find out in memorable detail where Rima had herself come from, as she related her story.

11

The year was 1944, and newborn Rima could scarcely get air to enter her fifty-five-week-old nasal passages, reach her lungs, and exit without a thunderous cough racking her infant body. Her tuberculosis made her an inflamed, mucous-secreting, fifteen-pound gob of humanity who had already wailed a lifetime of tears in her early childhood. Her story for the next quarter century was, at first glance, not a hero's. It did, however, trace a trail that led, over twenty-four years, to her being on the cusp of fulfilling the promise that others saw in her. She began to tell the gathered party what she remembered:

"As a teenage girl, I remember, oh how I wheezed. I lacked the respiratory capacity to play soccer, swim, dance ballet, or sing in the chorus. Yet I did have an outlet for my pain, suffering, and physically idle hours—I channeled all my energy into being driven. By sixteen, I had won a scholarship to study biomedicine, and I drew national attention from schools as a biomedical research prospect.

"When I got into university, my professors saw me as a sickly girl who had a combination of razorlike wits and the intense drive of someone who, understandably, approached my biomedical research with a personal stake in the outcome. It was true—from childhood through my teens into being a young lady on the edge of adulthood, I had sharpened my mind with a focus on molecular genetics that I dared to dream to could help me, and others like me.

"Unfortunately, some basic realities about my day-to-day life hadn't changed. Every day I still coughed up phlegm by the cupful from my congested lungs. Piercing aches and pains plagued my head and abdomen, even as I aced my graduate school entrance exams and began a PhD program at age eighteen. The university's greatest hospital clinicians looked at my case and soon had given me the available suite of antibiotics and other known therapies. My compromised and confused immune system, though, never gained traction toward steady improvement. My body began to suffer a side effect of the medication, an ion imbalance that played itself out in my muscles, causing contractions of my limbs. My care team prescribed me sedatives and painkillers for these cramps, but they continued to worsen until I became unable to walk without crutches. More medications were added to control my muscle spasms as the FDA approved them, further sedating my nervous system.

"After a year of this daily drug cocktail, I was a weakened specimen. I tossed and squirmed in a restless sleep until squinting myself awake at noon. I would collapse back into a desperate sleep by the first hints of sunset when my painkiller-numbed nervous system cyclically reclaimed my mind. This left me with a maximum of six hours a day for academic productivity, including the time and energy I had to spend on the necessities of eating and bathing. This was no way to do work, but I worked against all odds and disadvantages for my own cure. During the difficult year of 1966, my fourth year at the university, I gave in to being transitioned to a wheelchair.

"Discovering the cure for TB and true relief of its symptoms became even more my raison d'être, my holdout hope for a livable life. My path to a PhD dissertation became my clawing, crawling heave toward the finish line. My number of hours outside a delirium of foggy dreams each day fell to four, then a mere three.

"Yet, as though in defiance, one day I realized that my research inarguably reached a critical point. I had toiled for seven years to penetrate a genomic pharmacological question, and my research began to resemble that holy grail for doctorate seekers: an answer. It wasn't the full cure, but I was sure it was an important step in the biochemical pathway.

"When it dawned on me that my analyses and statistics were more than sufficient to prove to my colleagues and advisors in the field that it would lead to pharmacological treatments of juvenile TB, I requested a PhD dissertation defense appointment with my board of advisors. My board, ebullient, scheduled my defense for March 27, 1969, at an accommodating time of one p.m. This date was a mere two weeks after I had put together the evidence that I was ready for this. Why wait? Each day was more precious. Confident I was ready on paper and in the mind, I faced the ever-present question of my life up to that point: would I be ready and able in my body?

"I had developed a dear friendship with a sociology student named Shira. When Shira heard the news that my PhD completion was near, she knew it meant more to me than just an accolade or a career boost. Shira knew that my milestone was personal as well as academic and how much it meant that I would be one step closer to helping people—including myself—end their suffering.

"It was a Friday, with more than a week left before the dissertation defense. Shira took the opportunity to invite me, that very evening, to a very special and cosmopolitan wheelchair-accessible dance club called Wings 4 Wheels. Its DJs started jamming early in the evening to enable the chronically infirm to experience the beat before their energy waned for the night. This club had made itself famous for going beyond the municipally required accessibility codes, as well as pioneering some exotic-sounding natural health drinks not yet commonly offered in the 1969 nightclub scene, but which some had already discovered to be effective at rejuvenating ravaged tissues of the body.

"Notwithstanding these relevant perks, and not surprisingly, given my laser-like focus on research and development, I had never gone to this club before—not to dance, not to drink, and not for any other reason.

"In the steely blue wheelchair that gave me mobility, it was sometimes easy for me to forget that my limbs, my legs especially, were actually all there, anatomically sound, with nothing missing. My life's motto for nearly a decade had been 'Survive for research, research to survive,' and that hadn't left me with a lot of extra time for recreation or body awareness.

"Shira had really treated me to the complete works. She insisted that I wear, and then helped me don, my one pair of black high heels and my knee-length black-and-white swirl dress, both last worn in 1964. We rode in a handicapped-accessible limousine. When we arrived at our destination downtown, I was able to roll out onto the pavement sidewalk, facing the club's entrance. We slowly approached. The nightclub scene itself was so foreign, I was beside myself, murmuring in Shira's direction, 'I'd forgotten…it's like a different planet.'

"With Shira by my side, I rolled into the semidark club. We found ourselves sitting at a comparatively short bar designed with a space between each bar stool for a wheelchair. That meant that two friends could have a drink together, at even heights, even if one was chair bound. Ordering spring water with lemon and sea salt was not considered uncool here, which is exactly what we did.

"I noticed I unwound a little in this environment. I felt aware that I was alive in a way I hadn't allowed myself to be before. I was optimistic by nature; after all, what would have kept me going without my optimism? Gradually, I began to join Shira in acknowledging that this truly was a special occasion. I let myself start celebrating—turning the corner. The mere recognition of this small victory, with an uplifting musical beat and a friend committed to celebrating with me, provided me a space to let go of my self-applied pressure, if only for a moment.

"I hooked my arm into Shira's elbow and pushed my chair forward toward the dance floor, to which Shira happily responded with a step of her own in the same direction. Mmmm, the music! Somehow, the cramping wheeze in my chest abated a notch. The pain in my major muscle groups had somewhat diminished, and a sense of tension released. My toe, sheathed in my shiny black high-heeled shoe, began to tap against the wheelchair's foot stand.

"What I wanted more than anything at that moment was to get my high heels onto the dance floor itself, to feel the vibration of the music come through the floor and into the soles of my feet, so I lowered my foot off the foot stand down onto the polished wooden dance floor.

"The vibrations of the beat first permeated my lower foot and then traveled up to my ankle. I could feel the musicians' true sense of rhythm, driving forward incessantly; this dance song was a metaphor for the drive I incessantly applied to my scientific investigations, day after day. I was moved by the steady, tenacious beat. I identified with it. In the middle of the dance floor, I said to Shira: 'Help me stand up now,' and I put my arm around Shira's shoulder.

"I was standing and still tapping that toe. The vibration was now progressing all the way up my leg and reaching into my heart area, starting to fill my arms and even my collarbones. There wasn't any stopping this; mild and subtle as my movements were, I was dancing.

"Normally, there was a place along my midsection where abdominal cramps twisted me up in knots. But the vibration seemed to soothe and untie those knots, leaving my body more free to conduct energy. My wheezing seemed to be partially evaporating, and blocks in my energy flow were being cleared. As for my migraine, it was as though someone had opened the barred windows of a smoky attic, allowing fresh air to flow in and let the heavy staleness out.

"I then became keenly aware, in a way that was hard to understand and to explain, that a Herculean and marathon dissertation process—replete with physical and cognitive stress, struggle, and suppression of all thoughts and feelings that might stop me—had led me to experience this one moment, just as it was, the music's beat crescendoing into perfection. In a most unexpected way, my own health condition was creating within me a precipice over which I fell at that moment. I was passing through a gate into a reality I could have pretended to ignore—or I could allow myself to acknowledge. On one hand, I started to see that I had invested in the notion that molecular codes researched in laboratories were *the* source that could heal me. On the other hand, I was becoming able to experience the way my body felt as waves of joy and vibration undulated through my nervous system. I saw my investment in the laboratory as a blessing that had kept the flame of my hope alive and inspired my intellectual will, yet had also created obstacles to seeing other avenues of healing. Since I believed in the power of discovery and publication of knowledge, if I allowed myself to be open to what I was experiencing, I knew I would share the results and every aspect of it. And I would never again be the same.

"You would hardly believe the rest of the story if I told it to you forty times," Rima said to Gene, Hope, and Jim.

The Curtins had been alert and enthralled as they listened and gradually found out who Rima, the woman sitting in their living room, really was. They had no idea what had happened to her after the dance club. They did know one thing, however: Rima was sitting in their living room, glowing with easeful health.

After listening to this much of Rima's story, they certainly knew far more about her than that she was Don's wife, Nat's grandmother, and the woman who had appeared at their door. It was as though she had suddenly been transformed into a walking treasure trove of experience. Her grisly physical and mental challenges had sculpted her character and granted her discipline in her thoughts, and now she was a diamond. The obstacles she'd faced, and the effort that was necessary to overcome them, had caused personal power to rise from her depths and had strengthened her spine. Though they couldn't tell from her subtle manners, Rima's backbone was made of a resilient steel that stood as a proud testament to every member of humanity—for it was humanity: that of her university, that of Shira, that of Wings 4 Wheels, and that of the DJ—who had healed her and, further, awakened her as a beacon for other people needing healing to navigate by.

Rima's story was still not complete, and the Curtin clan wondered about the innumerable details that would follow about how she had gotten from there to here. One thing was clear: her story of a natural sort of healing, an alternative to the very medicine she was in fact studying, was not necessarily about nutrition, but about dance, rhythm, and vibration itself, a sort of immanent access to ecstatic gratitude that had been and remained her essential medicine.

"Immanent access to ecstatic gratitude" was a phrase that could describe the impression that Rima left on all the Curtins. For each of them, that phrase pinpointed the characteristic that allowed Rima, a survivor of a story like hers, to be sitting in their living room that day. Her strength of presence enlivened every discovery the Curtins had made that day about food and lifestyle choices that can help reverse diabetes. Through hearing Rima, Hope, Gene, and Jim each intuitively came to a point of understanding that in ecstatic gratitude, one may naturally find oneself attracted to natural foods, like the dance club for the disabled that served healthy smoothies. Indeed, Rima's presence intrinsically turned the Curtins' own nutritional discoveries into their own access to ecstatic gratitude. It was that kind of party.

—◊—

"Oh, really, Rima? So we wouldn't believe you if you told us what happened to you after that time in grad school—even if you told us forty times, you say?" Gene said.

"Why don't you try us?" Hope inquired.

So Rima resumed her story, and this time she shared with such a level of personality, vividness, and directness, that the gathering held their breath for every word.

12

"Well, that night in 1969—I still remember it like it was to-day—I had to be dragged off that dance floor, which I know sounds completely ridiculous for someone in my decrepit physical condition at the time. It's one hundred percent true, though. My dear friend, Shira—who was astounded, delighted, and also almost in tears—helped me eventually find my way to the exit of Wings 4 Wheels. The bartender saluted us with a wink and a thumbs-up as we exited through the automatically opening doors. Shira helped me up to my apartment. I hugged her, and though I said, 'Thanks for an amazing night,' I didn't have the conceptual framework or the vocabulary to describe how amazing it was. As a best friend, of course, whose teardrops were visible, I knew she understood on some level.

"Once I had collapsed on my bed, I dreamed in a most ephemeral reverie, a buzzy, full-bodied sleep in which I was immersed in nostalgia for a level of aliveness I had not experienced since my early childhood.

"The next morning—well, actually, after all the physical exertion, I slept till four p.m.—I awoke to a partially sad reality. For me to become a regular at Wings 4 Wheels was going to require a level of physical mobility and management of my energy that were far beyond my reach at that time.

"However, underneath my disappointment over the fact I couldn't be on the dance floor regularly lay the *most important thing about my condition*. Now that I had gotten one taste of the feeling of the music vibrating within my body's channels, it was living inside me. It had awakened something dormant, which would stay awake forever. I knew, despite my doubts, that I would be revisited by that feeling of being engulfed in living vibrations.

"If I couldn't go to Wings 4 Wheels, I would daydream about it. I would put myself in that 'frequency' mentally. I applied myself to this mental exercise completely, and being plenty good at it, I suddenly had a refuge that followed me everywhere I went. The healing vibrational sounds that had consumed me were accessible through simply closing my eyes and tuning my 'inner dial' to that blissful station.

"It was very individual, mind you. A night of 'dance' had stirred something inside me, even though my stiff and rigid body, which sat all the time, had hardly moved through space like a dancer's. I couldn't say I had 'healed' one iota in any measurable way, but I knew beyond a shade of doubt that the experience my body was undergoing was healing.

"I came to believe that—while it is certainly not through dance for everybody—almost everyone has something that can wake them up to an alive, healing inner reality. I'll never really know why my wake-up call came through dance. Someone else's call may come through the sudden grace of a loving relationship, while someone else's may come through a philosophical revelation. Someone else's may be an improbable proximity to a strike of lightning in an evening thunderstorm, while another might get it from an orator's rousing speech. For one, it will come from playing music, and for another, through planting bulbs and watching flowers bloom. I felt so comfortable and natural in this new inner vibration that it seemed as if all humans could have it, and I came to believe they could, a belief which has served me.

"Maybe my awakening catalyst came through dance because my original calling was to be a dancer, prior to falling so ill. I suppose a true calling has a way of getting to you in any way that is necessary. In my experience of the people I've met, almost all people have a calling. When the expression of one's calling emerges in his or her life, it is one of the most awe-inspiring illustrations of a human being's power that one can witness.

"So back to my journey. I know, to you, I'm left in my apartment, struggling to make it through the average day…and the next thing you know, I'm talking about the liberation of vast personal power. No, it was not an overnight miracle recovery.

"It was a day after night, after day after night, after day after night recovery.

"The first thing I did was re-create the space within myself to feel the energy of the Earth rising through my body. It took isolating myself from my work and my other thoughts for a bit. The first time, the very next day, it took so much mental force to block out all the other stimuli and feel the energy quivering in my body that I was deathly afraid that I would not find it again. But through my intention and my will, I did find it. I made a mental note, in the thickest mental marker I could find, so to speak, helping draw myself a map to that space. When I found it again, it was like soaking in a warm bath. Being able to go there and feel my body's life force was truly precious.

"Interestingly, the second day was easier than the first, and the third easier than the second. By fourteen days after the Wings 4 Wheels nightclub experience, calling up the vibrational experience was regular, less effortful, and almost spontaneous.

"The next step was really radical for me. What I had to start doing, I realized, was to begin realigning my environment with the vibrational experience that was now becoming a more regular, frequent, and stable inspiration.

"What I altered first turned out to be the easy stuff: I began listening to music that resembled the uplifting vibration from Wings 4 Wheels. Also, I changed the binder I used for my research papers to one that had an inspiring front cover image, because I looked at it so often. Instead of wasted space or an abstract equation, I could look at a beautiful painting that, to me, represented life, and health, and beauty.

"Then, of course, came the most complex and important part of my environment: people. Ugh…did I feel pressure to change that! Except for my dear best friend, who, if anything, I needed more of in my life—after all, she had taken me out that night, opening such an important door for me. Nothing about her had to change, and I often smiled about that. However, I had to deal with advisors, professors, colleagues, lab technicians, undergrads, interns, medical doctors, publishers, clerks. What kind of energy were they sending me?

"I gently approached one of my advisors to broach the subject of, well, perhaps talking to me with a more empowering energy. The way that turned out made me realize this was not going to be easy.

"You know, Hope, Gene, Jim…I could go on about that particular rough patch in my journey. Inside, my life force was turning back on and sending life into organs that I had given up on—save for a biomedical breakthrough—years ago. But nobody could see those changes yet. My only improvement visible on the outside, probably, was that I was in such a better mood. The profundity of my mind-body-spirit connection was lost on my fellow biomedical researchers.

"I knew I would never lose my respect for them, yet at the same time, I would have to move on from the laboratory.

"Not only did I ace my dissertation defense, but I had a really good time doing it. In the final section, I was describing what research the department could expect to see coming from my lab next. I told them exactly what experiments could be done, and they were very intrigued by the innovative experimental arrangement.

"Then I broke it to them that the experiments would have to be done by other researchers. In fact, my unique experimental lab setups were released with permission to be used by any lab on the planet. I, however, would be 'celebrating my successful doctoral defense'—at least, that's what I told them—with a year of leave. That was an unusual move for a researcher with the momentum of just having successfully defended a dissertation at such a prestigious institution. It was all the more shocking coming from me, since I was known to have not only the most personally driven work ethic, but also the least to do in terms of other activities.

"I expressed to my advisory committee that I certainly was not finished with my personal quest to discover the cure for myself and people with similar conditions. And I left it with my advisors just like that. What I didn't say to my committee, but did later share with Shira, was that the thought of me being the hardest worker in the lab because I had the least else to do, given my circumstances, smacked of an energy, one identified with my sickness that I could no longer be around. It would be too hard to explain...and my advisors were not ready for such an analysis. So I would have to go on leave.

"I began devoting my mind completely—not just for a few moments, but all my conscious hours—to cultivating the life force energy that had started rising inside of me. I was in this almost mystical realm from morning to evening. It continued in my dreams. Sometimes, I swear, I saw my apartment brightly lit by it at night.

"The uplifting music never ceased in my room; I was living in the sound healing version of 'The City That Never Sleeps.' Suddenly, my interaction with the outside world consisted of ordering the newest sacred music of the world CDs from Peru, Tibet, Ecuador, French Alpine monasteries, Thailand, Sweden, Ghana, India, Indonesia, the Lakota reservations, and more.

"Also, I would get signals in my meditative energy work—which is what I began to call it—that would tell me to look up an herbal dispensary, and sometimes I was practically given the name of the herb, all from inside. It made it so I hit it off with the herb salespeople very well, understood their specialized language, and I also, in fact, learned a great deal from talking with them. Sometimes Shira would do me a favor and pick up herbs around town, and sometimes an herb shopkeeper would drop them off at the front desk of my building and the doorman would greet me with them at the door. I boiled them in water and drank those teas in the agreed-upon amounts that

I had worked out with the herbalist, which almost always concurred with the intuitive sense I got from within.

"For added potency, I got an air ionizer and purifier and a few very large amethyst and quartz crystals to fill out the space. I had no timetable for when this life phase would end. It was *unstoppable*. I was really just trying to keep up with the reorganizing of my whole soul, it felt like. There were days I didn't even clearly distinguish between the time I woke up and the time I went to bed, I was in such a continuum of consciousness. That meant that, disregarding the whole idea of, 'Oh, poor, sick Rima, she sleeps eighteen hours a day,' it wasn't that I started to be awake for more hours. Rather, it was that the whole concept of being awake or asleep transformed, like a caterpillar transforming into a butterfly, instructed by the *Imaginal Cells* that activate in the cocoon, and a new concept came forth. Consciousness was along a spectrum, and I was going with it.

"My days passed with some intuitive sorting of the day into music experience, sitting; sound healing groove, standing and sometimes allowing movement to surge through me; boiling and drinking herbal teas; eating the superfoods and greens I was being guided to; and repeating.

"Soon, weeks turned into months, and what moved in me next was to write love letters, really naked stuff, to everyone and anyone who had ever harmed, offended, insulted, or just nudged me the wrong way. The forgiveness in my heart had to be expressed and known. I wrote letters of gratitude and appreciation to the people I loved—of course, those were some of the same people who had harmed me, I felt. Everything seemed to be a blessing, even the rough stuff I had experienced socially. That release and acknowledgment process itself took three months, while I continued as I was doing.

"It had been six months since this…*miracle* is the only word for it…began, and it was November. I remember that was the first time I didn't want to just feel the energy from heel to hip and slightly shimmy my leg. What was coming through then was an urge to begin stretching and bending my chair-stiffened limbs. This direction from my intuition came through strongly. Before I knew it, one morning, listening to the music after a tea elixir, my spine bent to the right, stretching the outside of my left hip. Suddenly, my left hand and arm soared upward to the sky and out from my chest. I was moving!

"I wanted to let extending movements happen frequently now, almost all the time. With Shira's help, I cleared a space in the apartment to create and keep a place for movement. Suddenly, things like yoga, tai chi, and qi gong were my beloved companions.

"Six more months passed, and it was May, the end of my one-year sabbatical. There was some stress on my mind, again, but for different reasons now. When I went to see my colleagues and professors again, what I was actually concerned about was that my funding for a year of sabbatical would not extend for more than exactly one year. I'd always done research out of a passion, not to pay the bills. But would I have no economic choice but to return to the lab?

"I was going to see my advisors, however, as a different me than before. As I'd expected, they asked me what was improving, what was changing, and how? What could I say? I just told them that what I was doing was, to my observations, working great.

"They said that, given the results they could see with their own eyes, it would seem that my treatment was working. I thanked them for their compliment. Then, sensing a blessing coming, I asked if I could take my postdoctoral work in the direction of my new techniques. To their eternal credit, they said yes, for as long as I wanted.

"It was perfect! I wouldn't need to be indoors in a lab, because every advisor and colleague had known me for so long and knew from experience doing research with me that if I were going to really make a change in my health, I, myself, my own person, was going to *be* the lab.

"I smiled inside. All I would have to do would be to keep notes. Could life have gotten any better?

"Now, I could write a novel about my story, all the things that made my transformation of health work for me—and some of the pitfalls I discovered by trial and error. But over the course of the next several years, I started making, frankly, incredible inroads into healing my body. I got out years of toxins from drugs, put in nutrients I had been deprived of for years, and my body responded, starting with reducing inflammation.

"The first way that I knew the inflammation had started to soothe was when I didn't feel as much pain. I reduced the pain medication gradually, until I really didn't need much. Also, my mucus level dropped considerably, and my respiratory system seemed to be improving. My abdominal aches dissolved. Even my excrement told me I was digesting things better. I spent more and more hours awake, and I stood more often. Soon I was standing every day.

"The day I could walk to my apartment door to let in a friend was a great milestone, one of the turning points. Then I could walk down the hall to the elevator, and that was huge, too. One day in 1974, I did just that, early in the morning: got a ride with Shira to the beach, rode home, and walked to the elevator and back home after sunset!

"I had become a woman I had never expected myself to be. I was a story in the campus newspaper—which seemed to take more notice than the scientific journals I used to publish in. Letting go of my frustration at the journals' failure to publish my articles on my progress was an emotional healing process for me. My forgiveness came eventually, and I got to have a love affair with a whole new kind of journal—the alternative press.

"In 1976, I did return to Wings 4 Wheels. At that point, of course, I walked in on my own two legs. Looking up from polishing the counter behind the superfood bar was the most handsome, beautiful, knightly presence: the same bartender who had given us a thumbs-up as Shira and I had floated out of Wings 4 Wheels seven years earlier.

"He was, of course, Don.

"He remembered me, as I remembered him. We were united in soul, soon united in body, and forever united in service and helping others."

13

As everyone processed Hope's story in silent astonishment, the sound of cleats clacking on a cement walkway interrupted their thoughts. *Click-clack-crikiteeclack* came the signature of shoes meant for the baseball diamond. *Click-clack-crikiteeclack*, approaching all the way up three concrete steps leading up to the front door of the Curtin home.

"Gramma, Gramma, where are you? Are you inside here?" yelled a young boy.

The gleam of Rima's smile intensified for her grandson, Nat.

And then came a different voice. "Hey, Nat, is Grandma in there, kiddo?" called Don, who had walked over to visit his neighbor.

In a voice that was strong and clear in a feminine way, far from the frail voice a seventy-year-old woman might be assumed to have, Rima responded with a joyful, "Oh, they're here!"

Still trailing his grandson by many steps, but trying to act as responsibly toward his neighbor as possible, Don called out instructions to Nat. "Leave the bat and cleats outside the front door, OK, Natty? Inside Gene and Hope's house is *not* a place for a Louisville Slugger."

As the boy huffed and puffed, hurriedly unlacing his baseball spikes on the porch, Don sauntered up to the front door. Gene, Hope, Jim, and Rima were still sitting in the living room. Jim, who apparently was taking a college literature class on tacky nicknames to go with his other academic subjects, said, "You know, I might as well call you 'Rima Joy.' It rings like a great name, and it's kind of perfect, you know, for who you are."

With friendly and witty sarcasm, Rima replied, "Thanks, Jim. I'm pleased to see that schools' emphasis on book learning hasn't clubbed improvisation and spontaneity out of our bright young minds!"

"Nope, I haven't been booked to death yet."

Hope was enjoying watching her son banter with her impressive neighbor, and the corners of her mouth curved upward at the pun.

As Don made it into the house at last, Gene responded the way a player does when he sees his coach come into view. He sat a little taller, a little more at attention, and tried to shelve any mental distractions.

Meanwhile, Jim, who was meeting Don for the first time, said, "This must be 'Don the Health Man,'" in an obvious eponymous stretch.

Don was obliging. "Take it from me, Jim—and by the way, nice to meet you; I've heard good things about you from your father—one successful man to a successful man to be: the ability to think on your feet and incorporate humor is going to help you so awfully much in your life. I mean, in my own life and Rima's, it's about being perceptive of moments that arise spontaneously and marking these moments in your awareness so they can reach their full life-changing potential—including using silly names if you choose to." Don smiled and added, "Heck, that's what we're doing here right now. If you think about it, it's like fresh versus canned food..."

He wasn't finished with his entrance speech, apparently. "Results come far more rapidly," he continued, "from what's fresh, whether it's your food ingredients, your conversations with people, the material you present to your colleagues in life, or the thoughts you entertain about the world. For example, I've always been intrigued by the fact that plants are essentially regulated as to how long they can use yesterday's sunlight—not very long. The light they need has to be just eight minutes old—eight minutes, of course, being how long it takes light to get from the sun to the Earth. Not a plant on this green Earth can live long on yesterday's sunlight."

Don continued rolling like a stream. "Take Rima—she keeps her inspiration fresh through dance and lots of other practices. I don't know if she's told you yet, but she's got a life story about being spontaneous that will *knock your socks off*!"

Right then, size-four kids' socks flew across the room at Don, out of Nat's right hand.

"Thanks for the illustration, Nat. Right on cue! Glad you're paying attention," Don said to an uncontrollably giggling Nat.

"Take music, too—the music we dance to is the music we're listening to right then, right?" Don continued. "Do you dance to music you were hearing yesterday? How funny would you look doing that? Now, Rima got in touch with the rhythm of the moment one night, and it transformed her life, because that practice that she found... she kept doing it!"

"You're a little *after* the moment yourself, Don," Rima cleverly teased. "Life-Supporting Nutrition 101 at Curtin University is already in session, and someone was truant from the opening lectures!" This elicited the laughter of Gene, Hope, and even Jim, who felt familiar enough to be jocular with Don despite having only just met him.

Don had to chuckle self-effacingly, and was unperturbed as he spoke. "You know how people are always studying and investigating to prove theories? Well, it is true what they say: theories generate results when they are put into practice. Much more useful is: theories generate *the results we want* when they are put into practice, fully embedded in the context and flow of the dance of our own lives. It's like—what was her name, honey?—that's right, Gabrielle Roth, who invented the 5Rhythms practice. And we keep coming back to this: it works when we are present in and responsive to the moment. Without that improvisation—what do I like to say happens? Do you remember what we were talking about, Natty? Rust and...Natty, what was it, rust and...?"

"Dust! Rust and dust!" Nat exclaimed.

Gene, who had been quietly absorbing all the new information for a while, at that moment spoke up toward Jim's direction: "Son, I do have to say, spontaneity was fairly rare in my life up until the recent changes. A bit of uncommon spontaneity was what allowed me and Don to meet, actually. It let me be accepting of the unpredicted, unexpected appearance of Don's surprising message for me, delivered through the unusual means of slipping a photograph into the morning paper. Since I got my prosthesis, so many things have occurred to change up my routine, adding spontaneity. Even the idea of having this study party here at home: it is totally unprecedented, and not very long ago, I would never have believed it would be happening."

"If I may add, just by her showing up, Rima totally demonstrated a similarly spontaneous side of her," Hope said.

This led Gene to muse, "All this that has taken place, it has taken place in the moment. My accident, even, was spontaneous, as accidents are. But before my accident, when was the last time we had a gathering of family and neighbors, with Jim home from college, spending time in peace and happiness? When? Can't remember? Exactly. And now it's happening. So, look, I've stopped lamenting the accident now; I've stopped judging it as good or bad. It was an event. It was a part of life, which shifted the rhythm of the song of my life. Living is kind of like being a drummer, staying on beat after beat in a rhythm we call life."

"Well, that's not bad. But I'm going to one-up you all in spontaneity," said the young and sprightly Jim, looking up from texting on his cell phone. "Right about..."

Ding dong.

"...now!" Jim grinned, already in the act of bounding to the front door.

"Hey, Dana!" he said as he opened the door.

"Hi, Jimmy! It's good to see where your folks live, and good to see you!"

"It's good to see you, too," Jim said, and they hugged at the door-way. "Now come in, I'll introduce you."

"Sure I'm not intruding?"

"Naw, come, come in!"

Jim escorted Dana down the hallway to the living room and an-nounced, "Everyone, this is Dana." And then Jim turned toward his extra-special college friend and said, "This is my mom and dad… and these are their new friends, Don and Rima, and their grandson, Nat."

"Real spontaneous, Jimmy," Don teased. "You got us with your instant messaging. Well, it sure seemed spontaneous to us, you show-man! I'll say, though, I am convinced that you understand what we have been talking about, pertaining to spontaneity, and I'm confi-dent and pleased that you are carrying that into your life."

"True, true." Jim nodded. "And everyone, I invited Dana because I am honestly proud of this moment in my family—we are at our best tonight. Frankly, you aren't acting like 'my old folks,' but are actually being 'with it,' like you're alive inside the times. I'm learning lots of stuff from each of you here. It's really cool.

"I've been wanting to introduce you to Dana for a while now. She's someone who's become really special to me. And this was the moment I chose. I love you, Mom, and I love you, Dad, and I've been scared since your accident, really scared." Jim paused as he felt tears surge up.

"Mom, when you asked me to bring certain books home from the university library, I didn't know exactly what it was for, but I was cautiously excited. It seemed you might be getting really motivated to keep Dad around for long enough so I can have him in my life as I grow older and important things in my life happen. I said to Dana that tonight, my family might be acting like the family that I know they are. It turned out you're being special in all the ways I can imagine, really a family that stands together and shares resources with one another. You've brought awesome neighbors over, too. I am definitely proud to introduce Dana to you. 'Cause she's so cool, you know," Jim said, wanting to flatter Dana. "I gotta have a cool family to introduce her to."

Awkwardly, Jim completed his expression of emotion. Father, mother, son, and dear friends were witnessing the profound impression that they were having on each other. Gene saw that his son had grown up to a new level. Hope squeezed Gene's hand and wanted to hug Jim.

"Pleased to meet you, Dana. I can already tell you are a special person and a special woman to Jim," Hope said with admiring, instant affection.

"And Jim, what a stunningly touching introduction to your friend. Oh, my goodness!" Rima said, to nods around the room.

Dana was cutely collegiate-looking and was wearing a red knee-length dress and brown, knee-high, thick, scrunched socks. Her wavy medium-brown hair snaked away from a smooth, rich complexion and a wide, white smile, her eyes shining behind her wire-framed spectacles.

Dana was a poised young woman. Though she could have been embarrassed, she chose to embrace the beautiful moment.

She scanned the room, seeing the faces and feeling the presences of the people gathered. She read the large presentation papers that were taped to the walls, and glanced down at Jim's recent texts on her mobile device. Attentive by nature to the ideas in the space around her, Dana wanted to quickly shift from being introduced to belonging there, without an awkward acclimatization period.

After a moment, Dana queried the room at large, "So, I'm hearing that you've been talking about spontaneity, the joy of movement and dancing, and eating as nature intended in the company of ones we love, to nourish the so-called roots of our body, our intestines. I'm looking at this from the outside, but is that a basic summation?"

Don said, "Well, I'm glad you got that—and nice real-time texting, Jimbo, so Dana could be in on the conversation even without being here for most of it. And that, frankly, is where we've got to take this conversation, in my opinion, for my healing."

"Where?" Gene asked.

And then, suddenly, he began answering his own question. "The plots of our lives really begin when there is action."

Gene, whom his wife had always known as a "man of action," at that moment was in the process of gaining a greater understanding of action than he had ever had before, especially when it came to his health.

Dana added, "In other words, 'Where is thought if it never leaves the thinker?' That's what my professor likes to say."

"Exactly. You're both onto it," Gene said. "If I'm going to use the knowledge we've raised today, it's going to have to leave this room. It's going to have to be shared with others so my life can, you know, integrate this."

Sensing his own energy, Gene finally added, "I'll tell you what else I'm on to, as the man of action of the house. This study-in is officially in need of a break; it's far from over, though—Rima, I've got lots more to learn from you, and Dana, I am so honored to meet you, and I would like to spend some time getting to know you. Jim, thank you so much for raiding the library. Don, you're a spark, man. Nat, keep swinging with your eye on the ball. And Hope, dear one, thank you for believing in the possibility for today to even happen. I have taken in a lot today. It's a lot of amperage for my circuitry, as I would put it as an electrician. So let's put school on a break, and let's mingle, chitchat, schmooze with each other, whatever. I thank you from the bottom of my heart. Now, if there's not too many crates of books in the way, I am going to walk into the kitchen, start looking in the cupboards, thinking more about what would be pleasurable and healthful to eat, getting ready to call it a night."

—✵—

The mingling continued for a while, Rima enthralling people with the story of her journey from illness to well-being through rhythm, energy, motion, and the emotions and foods she entertained most often, also known as mental and physical hygiene (which she pointed out, just for that night, could be spelled "Hi, Gene"). Dana, as the night went on, had her opportunity to settle in and get to know people in a natural flow, the surprise of her dramatic introduction finally subsiding and being left in the rearview mirror as nothing but an auspicious start to a positive relationship with Jim's family.

Gene bumped into Jim on his way down the hallway. Jim had been waiting for him.

"Hey, Dad, check this out!" He handed his dad a cell phone.

"What?"

"It's yours! I got a great deal on a no-contract cell phone. The first month is on me. If you want to renew, the number is taped to the back of the phone," Jim offered.

"For what? Oh, I get it, if anything happens to me, it'll make you feel better if I have a phone," Gene said.

"No, I just thought I'd text you the play-by-play in real time from my Human Development class. The prof's a real dynamic lecturer. Texting it to someone outside class in the real world helps me learn, you know, by making sure I keep my mental dialogue on the subject relevant," Jim replied.

"OK, kiddo, thanks. This texting thing you do—at least it really works for you with Dana, it seems," Gene said. "I'm glad to see you happy with someone, and thank you for bringing her to meet us."

They hugged each other then, and in the silence, both absorbed the sentiment that they felt for each other.

Don and Rima understood it had been a long day of discovery and inspiration for Gene, especially when it came to processing information under pressure. There is stress in having a physical condition that makes some simple movements challenging. Further, it is tiresome to constantly be concerned about falling down a slippery slope of worsening health if one makes the wrong choices. Therefore, Don and Rima wanted to make their exit in a manner that would take up as little time and space as humanly possible. When they had finished—and thoroughly enjoyed—sharing heartfelt appreciation and talk of their worlds with their hosts, they gathered up Nat and anything that he had left disordered and then slipped unassumingly down the warm hallway toward the front foyer. From a distance down this hall, Don turned around, made reassuring eye contact with Hope, and gave her an admiring nod. Rima, capturing Gene's visual attention, spoke encouraging volumes with a wide smile that spread across her face, and mouthed something that Gene interpreted as a playful "You rock!" but he was too tired by that point to confirm it.

At the front door, Don helped Nat tie his cleats and pick up his kid-sized twenty-inch Louisville Slugger.

Gene was still gazing warmly after his departing neighbors. He felt an inexplicable sense of closer friendship with them. Gene's gaze fell on the baseball bat that young Nat was picking up with all his arm strength as Don helped tie his shoe. Half squinting, Gene was able to barely make out a pattern that he didn't recognize on the sweet spot of the baseball bat.

Was it a new logo from the sporting goods industry? It appeared to be pressed onto the hardwood with permanent dark wood stain, as though it had always been there, yet it was so unique. The pattern looked like seven baseballs or other round objects in orbit around a center sphere.

Simultaneously, as Hope was watching Don lean down to help Nat ready himself to go home, she thought she saw something poking out of Don's back pocket that looked like a chisel, though she didn't make much of it even though its reflective twinkle was the last object she saw as Don and Rima escorted Nat out into the night, homeward bound.

Eventually, each of the guests made their way toward their resting places for the night, Jim enthusiastically doing the same with Dana.

14

After everyone had left her home, but before brushing her teeth and winding down, Hope had excused herself to tend to her husband by preparing a breakfast and lunch for him for the next day, to the best of her current ability, worthy of what he had discovered and helped her discover about nutrition and health that evening. She had been collecting tasty vegetables, low-glycemic fruits, and high-mineral and good-fat nuts and seeds—and mental notes on how to prepare them—realizing she'd be ready to use them eventually. Tonight was the first night of "eventually," even though she was going on as much intuition as proper memory of the preparation techniques.

First, Hope blended some almonds and water, and she strained out the pulp. Then she took that liquid and poured it over two cups of chia seeds. A little vanilla powder, and that was done.

Next, she placed a cup each of sun-dried tomatoes, sunflower seeds, and sliced green peppers in the food processor, and then she added a pinch of sea salt. She processed that until it was kind of like a thick sauce. Then she tore leaves of different kinds of lettuce and kale into salad-sized pieces and chopped some cucumbers. Into two glass travel containers she divided both the salad and the thick sauce. She licked the food processor blade and smiled. Tasty. That was done. Breakfast and lunch for both her and Gene.

Hope welled with pride at providing herself and her husband with this nutritious food for the next day as she wrote a note to Gene describing what was available. She left it on the kitchen counter.

As Hope replaced the pen and notepad in the sliding stationery drawer, she sensed her hand brush against something rough and organic-feeling. *In this drawer, what could that be?* she thought. As she found she could easily grip this object with her fingers, she took it out of the drawer.

She held the unexpected object, looked at it, and slid it around in her fingers. It was rough, like a piece of limestone, with a surface texture punctuated by minimalist lettering carved into it. Hope felt the rough, curved surface of the stone as she kept her gaze fixed upon it. It was a tannish-red hue, like sandstone. It was of standard weight for a stone, perhaps a little heavier than one might guess for its size. It was far more substantial than pumice, less dense than basalt, a volcanic rock.

The letters were neither machine engraved nor rudimentary, but had seemingly been carefully made by hand. As she read the inscription on the stone, Hope was stunned by the relevance of what was written there to the rejuvenating meals for herself and Gene she had just enthusiastically prepared.

Hope turned her eyes up to look at the chef work she had done, then returned her gaze to her palm and the discovered treasure it held, associating the two. Simultaneously, she was flooded with confusion as to the origins of this stone and a peculiar state of giddiness, as though touched by a mystic intelligence that had joined her as she walked into the unknown realms of advocating for her and Gene's health, then and into the uncharted future.

Though Gene was already in the bedroom changing for the night, Hope wanted to share the magic of this stone surprise with him. She arranged an even greater unexpected discovery of the stone for Gene than she herself had made. Retrieving the smallest glass container in her kitchen, a travel box for something the size of a cookie or a brownie, or possibly a bar of soap, she placed the stone into it. Then she opened the refrigerator door, kneeled down, reopened the larger lunch-sized container that held the salad and sauce, and hid the stone, in its smaller box, underneath the chopped cucumbers, just off to the side of the sauce.

After closing all the boxes and the refrigerator door, Hope noticed her note on its orange square of paper, ready for Gene in the morning, and thought, *I wonder what Gene will say when he sees everything tomorrow...*

—៣—

"My man of action," Hope whispered to Gene teasingly when their heads finally came to rest on their pillows together. "A man who understands the Zen-like academic koan, 'Where is thought if it never leaves the thinker?' What does this mean for you, dearest?"

"Actually, right now, all thought *has* left the thinker, so I don't know what it means for me," Gene said from a very right-brained place as he pressed PLAY on the CD player, out of which began to seep a remastered, classically romantic groove that both he and Hope had always loved to listen to. The rhythm instantly heightened their enjoyment of the view through the windows overlooking the valley and the sensation of the sheets under their bodies. "I'm going to let the beat of the song of our lives tell me everything I need to know," Gene said as he smiled at Hope in the night.

15

Morning was still breaking when Gene awoke from a dream of huge bright lights drawing a current of energy up from a power source through a system of switches that rose into the highest habitable altitudes. Hope was still sleeping, so he kissed her head with affection.

This particular morning, Gene felt a determination to do something that he had not done since the accident, and that was to drive somewhere alone, walk around alone when he got there, and drive back alone. For thought to leave the thinker, he had to get into action, after all. With a little kick still left in his old hips, Gene flipped himself upright. He fitted the stub of his right foot, more easily and with less subconscious shame than the day before, into the prosthetic two-thirds of that foot. As he'd gotten used to, he shuffled around in his morning routine until the stump of his foot settled into place. By the time he arrived in the kitchen, Gene was walking with only a barely perceptible hobble.

And there, Gene saw Hope's loving note to him on the counter island, which directed him into the refrigerator to the waiting assemblage of sure-to-be-delicious, vibrant, rainbow-colored, whole, and healthy fare she had prepared.

Little did he know about the stone…

As Gene inserted the keys into the driver's-side door of his Corvair, he noticed a small rectangle on the windshield. It was a textured aqua blue, with a sheen. Surprised to see anything at all on his car, Gene's first thought was that somehow he'd gotten a traffic ticket. As ridiculous as that thought was, since he was parked at his own house, it did, however, get Gene to move as quickly as he could to reach around and pinch the envelope between his fingers. He tried to pull it off the windshield, but it snapped back, as if to say, "Hey, don't just discard me; I am something important."

A crimson rubber band was holding the aquamarine mini envelope tight to the windshield wiper. Gingerly sliding the band down the wiper blade with his outstretched right hand, Gene finally detached the card-like envelope from the loop of the rubber band and a clip, drew it closer in, and examined it.

Hope usually handles greeting cards, Gene thought.

But this day—and the actions he would take in it—were already "his," he had decided. Hope remained sleeping, and heck, what was wrong with doing something a little out of the ordinary, like opening a cutely colored card envelope?

A single cream-colored card glided out, with raised embossing around the border. The card simply said:

Happy discovery journey!

"Really? On my car? Keepin' the party going, huh, guys?" Gene mused somewhere between dismissing the card as a random oddity on one hand, and on the other hand considering the possibility of appreciating someone's continued support.

He headed downhill, toward the flats of town. The sky was the gray color of predawn. A morning chill was in the air, but the weather was otherwise mild.

In his prime, Gene remembered, he was lighting up this city—literally. One of the best contracts of his career was the AM Tower on Fifth Street, one of the tallest in the municipality. That job had been completed going on eighteen years ago. Jim had been just a toddler—it was a workaday life—and Gene's family was being built little by little, day by day. Gene wanted to revisit that stretch of memory lane.

The building site's security guard back in the '90s had known Gene well, for both men had arrived before sunrise to begin work many times. It had been years since Gene had visited, and the security guard had changed. Gene recognized by the uniform, however, that the same security firm was still keeping the building safe.

Gene parked at the curb in a one-hour parking spot, hoping for a good bit of time inside the building. He walked toward the front entrance with measured, even steps, as he more confidently placed his feet down. The guard's name badge said Brian Johanson.

Gene greeted him. "Good morning, Brian. Gene Curtin. How are you?"

"Good, sir, thanks, and you?"

"Listen, Brian, I used to be the senior electrician for this building. I knew the security guard back then, Pat Delaney."

"Really?" Brian replied. "No kidding? Pat is the company's senior manager of building security accounts. I didn't know he'd guarded at all. And this building!"

"Well, is that right? I had no idea he'd become a manager like that," Gene said pensively on a bit of a trip down memory lane. "Shows where you can go, doesn't it, Brian?"

Brian smiled with an affirming nod, taking a moment to get in touch with his aspirations.

"Brian, I want to show you something." Gene bent down, lowered his sock, partially lifted his foot out of his loosely tied shoe, increasing the quizzical and dramatic experience for the young guard, and revealed to Brian a patch of the fiberglass prosthetic foot.

"This happened a year after I retired from running the commercial electricity company that I founded. Diabetes got me that day. But I wanted to get back up inside this building, where, when I was finished installing the fuse boxes, wiring, and switches, I used to look over the town and ponder what actions to take in my business and my life. I've got some thinking about my actions to do again. Do you think you could let me into the building?"

"I truly respect you, Mr. Curtin. But you want to get into this building, with no official business here today, to ponder what actions to take in life? I wish I could, sir, but I cannot let you in," Brian responded genuinely.

"All right, all right…I understand," Gene said.

Brian then replied, "But I do suspect that Mr. Delaney would be happy to talk to you. Here's my card; call the company's main number and just ask for him."

Gene said, "Thanks. I might do that."

Section 2:
The Three Foundational
Principles

16

Gene turned the key in the ignition. He sat back in the driver's seat again, in a place where he and Hope had made many memories that now popped up in his mind. After a slow and misty-eyed drive westward toward Riverbank Park, he parked in the vacant parking lot, got out into the fresh air, and walked under the verdant canopy of walnut trees, which sheltered doves that were beginning to awaken from slumber in the nests above his head.

To Gene and Hope, Riverbank Park was not just a place where Hope's habitat restoration project had been saved by a keen-eyed botanist's call for a soil change. Nor was it merely the site where Gene, liking to think of himself as a behind-the-scenes minor celebrity, would light up the city's festive holiday displays. People would flock from all directions to view the displays—all the way from the surrounding counties. Gene valued having had the opportunity to help bring magic to people's lives, especially to the children, who were awed at the brightness.

But no, that wasn't all. Riverbank Park was where Gene had taken Hope on their first date. His desire for her had been triggered by the way she sounded, smelled, looked, and, most of all, the way he felt in her presence.

It was where they had their first kiss and where Gene had knelt down to propose to Hope that she marry his hardworking, ambitious self.

Further, it was their favorite place to take slow walks while Hope was pregnant with Jimmy and also to expose their son to the outdoors and stroll as a family. During the intermittent silences of those walks, between talking with Hope and playing with Jimmy, it was this place that enabled Gene to reflect on life and consider his actions and their consequences for the Curtin family at large, more than anywhere else.

Riverbank Park was the sacred ground of their lives.

Losing a foot was one way to end a chapter of life and begin a new one, Gene mused. Walking on a prosthesis was not what he would have imagined would be his defining life change as he entered retirement, but it had begun to pan out as quite an eye-opener. Gene had already been a part of things—a nutrition home study session, for God's sake—that would never have transpired had he and his family not been subjected to a drastic wake-up call ,and had his family not put health and healing so urgently at the center of their lives. Yet up to this point, Gene had been in the unfamiliar and double-edged position of following the lead of others in his family. He was touched that they'd rallied to his side in these vulnerable times, yet he feared the very notion of no longer being the driver of action in his family, in his domain. Even worse than losing his foot would be losing his grip on his initiative and the power to affect the direction of his life.

This morning excursion had helped him come to a settled awareness of what he yearned for in the new chapter of his life, a distinct chapter from the old one. He would be mainly fulfilled if he could once again feel like a man of action, while acknowledging that he'd have to share aspects of his health that he never had before.

Just as he had done in his electrician business to gear up for a new project, Gene needed to take stock of what he had learned. The previous night had been brilliant, but here, in this partly cloudy, gray, pink, and increasingly blue morning, what was the essence that stuck in Gene's consciousness, like the proverbial spaghetti sticking to a wall?

Since they'd been written in block letters by his loved ones on a flip chart, he did remember three things, which had been gleaned from the books that they'd studied into regular, everyday language:

The unit of health is the household.

Food flips the switches of our health.

Our intestines are our roots.

Fortunate me, having this family, Gene mused.

Yet as sweet as it is to have the love and some health and nutrition revelations from my family, I am at a complete loss as to what to do with them.

In practicality, if I'm going to recover tissue function in my body, I need a regimen, Gene thought in a moment of clarity.

When I was wiring building systems, I needed to know the big picture, what the building was for, what its purpose and intention was. That provided context for the job. Likewise, for my mind to really embrace new practices as a healthy regimen, I also need a base understanding of the system, something to lend context to my new regimen.

Seeking the greater understanding that would help him get results that would keep diabetes far away from his body and his family, Gene watched the river pass by the point on the bank where he was standing. Constantly flowing, the water molecules never stopped their journey, yet the river never disappeared. One water molecule replaced the last, every second of the day, every day.

Gene looked a little more deeply into the water. He pondered, what was similar and what was different between the flow of electric currents and the flow of water currents. Letting his gaze settle on parts of the river bottom that were muddy, he wondered if that same mud had been on the river bottom the day before. Probably at some point, a day or a week before, that mud, although it looked the same, had been made of entirely different wet dirt particles and had been replaced.

These seemingly random associations in Gene's mind about things getting replaced continued until he got to people. People, too, get replaced. Like that security guard, Pat, who Gene knew from his days of working in that building. He had been replaced by Brian, whom he had met earlier that day. Maybe Pat would have let Gene into the building had he still been around, yet moving out of the guard job and getting replaced so he could move up surely couldn't have been a bad thing for Pat.

And then Gene's mind came to center on himself. After he had sold his business, the company named Curtin's Circuits still did electrical work, but the person at the helm had changed, or more precisely, had been replaced through an exchange of energy.

Then it struck him—everything gets replaced: water molecules, mud particles, people. And in every case Gene could imagine, that was a good thing. Rivers flow, mud moves along so as not to clog up streams, and people move up or move out to make room for others.

And then one thing he'd read during the study session came back clearly into his memory: the cells within the body get replaced, too.

"If my cells turn over and get replaced," Gene said matter-of-factly to the gushing stream, the only one listening besides himself, "then I get a new start with my body!" The second half of that sentence came out with much more gusto and the excitement of promise.

Well, he thought, *technically, as I read, I get a new start every seven years, when the body's cells go through a complete replacement cycle. What I have today is the opportunity to work with the idea that, if I stay focused for seven years, I will experience a new start. And that sure beats thinking I have to do total repairs of my currently damaged cells. My body will replace them for me. I've got a firing-and-hiring-happy HR department for my own cells and tissues. That's pretty cool.*

On the scratch pad that Gene still kept in his pocket, left over from his electrician days, which had required speedy, handy notes, he wrote: Foundational Principle for Health #1: Cellular Replacement.

Indeed, continuing to contemplate the fact that his body would replace his cells for him, Gene realized something else.

The body is going about replacing cells, doing what it does. It's just doing it. I don't have to convince it. The body doesn't moralize. It is living organic matter that follows a certain biological blueprint. At the cellular level, it responds as it responds to input. Inputs to the cells come from their environment of plasma and lymph fluids. The condition of this environment is determined by many factors, including stress levels of the person, movement and exercise, diet, cleanliness of the physical environment, what the mind is thinking, what emotions the person is feeling, genetic factors, amount of sleep, age, and more.

So, then, if the body is made up of organic cells, tissues, organs, energy, and systems, it is up to the consciousness of the human being to determine the body's input and thus, very likely, its results.

On the notepad, Gene wrote: Foundational Principle for Health #2: Body Consciousness.

Gene was still deep in thought as gold started creeping over the horizon to the east, creating a sparkling effect both upon the river and the modern buildings within his field of vision. He pondered:

Let's see—my cells replace themselves and, frankly, those little guys in and of themselves don't have a care of their own for what kind of cell comes after them.

Who is left to care, then?

Who is it that cares? It's me! If there's one thing a man of action has to be, it's passionately caring for the consequences of action and inaction. Yes; yes, I do care. It's not my body that really gives a darn—the body simply has its responses that impact me in beneficial or detrimental ways—it's me who cares.

He had to let that one sink in for more than a second. *Who cares?*

"It's me!" Gene shouted as dawn broke. "If anyone has a horse in this race, it's me! It's my ride, and it's on me!"

Kind of like calculating how to step down the distribution of one hundred and ten volts so that it illuminates a string of lights at forty watts, Gene did a little calculation within himself: Caring distributed over action = choosing.

The thinker inside Gene then began interpreting the balance of this equation:

So, if the action of caring is choosing, what is it I really get to choose?

Let's see, yesterday I became aware that, like these very walnut trees, I, too, am nourished from the roots, which in the case of human beings are our intestines. Hope taught me that. I also know from my son's research that the unit of health is the household, and things are changing remarkably toward a very supportive direction there, I'm proud and happy to say.

And I found, as only an electrician could, that food flips the switches of health. The body's system is not entirely different from an electrical system. The expression of the genes we are born with can be switched on and off, and food and lifestyle are switches for many of these genes. The more genes that are switched on, the higher-functioning the epigenetic expression, and the more genes that are switched off, the lower.

With an unfurrowing of his brow, it suddenly dawned on Gene that if his body consciousness was determining the replacement of his cells, then he was essentially the captain standing on the bridge of a ship. Operating the ship from the bridge involves not just one switch, but an entire switchboard and throttle at the captain's disposal. The captain decides the route the ship is taking and can point the bow in any direction on the compass that he chooses. Gene experienced a thrilling Captain Ahab moment for himself as he realized, *Basically, I've got three hundred and sixty degrees of freedom to navigate to get my body to the health I want. Sure, there are icebergs, capes, and continental shelves to look out for—but nobody here but me gets to steer. And I get to choose the mates and advisors on board, as well.*

The gem within that discovery then surfaced for Gene: *Health is not about "sick or well." It is beyond "cured or not cured." I'm not a "success" or a "failure."*

Even "dead or alive," I have to see with a completely different meaning. As the saying goes, "I die a thousand times before my death," and as a guy who passed out with his foot on the accelerator, I finally get it: poor health and good health is a continuum. It's more of a process, almost an artistic one, definitely a creative one. A process of moving across a wide range with the direction, speed, and style being up to me: I'm either deteriorating or rejuvenating.

At that moment, with the sun slowly cresting over the distant horizon, Gene penned: Foundational Principle for Health #3: Perpetual Motion on the Whole-Health Creative Continuum.

17

"**A**ll you'd have to do is provide me two security guards for the football semifinal game. Middletown High is so excited to not only be in the semis, but also to be hosting our first game this big in a quarter century. You provide the absolute best and you price your services honestly. You're a local guy, too. Whaddaya say, Pat?" Principal Jake Quibly said.

"I'll have to think about it," Pat Delaney said.

"I thought you'd have an answer right away," Jake said. "I really don't have any reason to meet with you if you don't. When do you think you'll let me know? Our game is a week from Saturday."

"Jake," Pat said, "I'd like you to go back and think about the proposal I made to you before, and respond to me before I decide about the big game's security next Saturday. No response, no True Security. I'd love to provide our services, and I know this game means a lot for the community, even for my own sons and daughters. But my answer is still, no--not until I hear you address my ideas for the school specifically—it's that important."

After a pause, Pat continued, "And I thank you for understanding, Jake."

Jake sat and shook his head back and forth slightly. He couldn't for the life of him, even after several conversations, wrap his head around why Pat was still making insistent demands about what was served in the cafeteria—something about "quality ingredients" and stuff—in order to ink a *football game security* deal. All Jake could keep thinking again and again was that Pat was one weird and unusual executive.

"Take care, Pat," said a slightly numb-sounding Jake.

"OK, bye for now," Pat said, ending with, "I still hope to hear from you," and hung up the phone.

—⚬w—

"What business, or reason, would I have to see Pat Delaney?" Gene wondered, muttering aloud. "Aw, I'll just tell him congratulations for reaching the top."

He took the business card out of his jeans pocket. Then, thinking, *How appropriate! My son has good timing with electronics*, he realized he had his new cell phone in his jacket pocket and dialed the main company line.

"True Security, how may we serve you?" the receptionist answered.

"Yes, my name is Gene. I'd like to speak with Pat."

"Pat Delaney?"

"Yes, Pat Delaney."

"I'll transfer you to Mr. Delaney's office."

"Pat Delaney's office, can you hold, please?" Pat's administrative assistant said.

"I haven't talked to Pat in seventeen years, so what's another few minutes?"

"Please hold,"

The hold music sounded as though it could have been from the iPod collection of a youngster Jim's age. *Hmmm, maybe this is what my son does for money to afford new cell phones*, he joked to himself.

"Thank you for holding," came the assistant's voice on the line.

"Yes, this is Gene Curtin, C-u-r-t-i-n," Gene said, feeling ridiculous. "I'd like to speak with Pat. Oh, you can tell him we knew each other from the AM Tower about seventeen years ago."

"And is this a scheduled call, Mr. Curtin?"

"Maybe you can tell him that Brian Johanson scheduled it," Gene said.

"Mr. Delaney's first appointment hasn't come in yet. I'll see if he is available to speak. Please hold."

Not bad, Gene thought. *So it's true…possibly…what they say about the early bird. Another lesson learned.*

To Gene's surprise, he heard, "Gene, this is Pat. How are you doing? This is unbelievable!"

"Well, hey, Pat, wow! I didn't expect to actually talk to you today. It's a bit disorienting, like time has become disjointed, with so many years gone by, and so many changes. I mean, just look at you! And with no appointment…"

"You know, let me tell you something, Gene—no, better tell it to you in full, in person. Are you in town?"

"At Riverbank Park actually, yes. Up early for a walk. Unusual for me, but true."

"Oh, man, that's awesome. That's part of what I'm talking about!" Pat exclaimed.

"What's part of what you are talking about?" Gene tried to catch up.

"Listen, I've got someone coming in five minutes, and then I just found out my ten o'clock, a local job, um, isn't ready to meet with me. You want to meet up here?"

"Sure, where?"

"One hundred seventy Furniss Street, suite two hundred. I'll let the lobby and front desk know," Pat said.

"Well, I'll see you then."

"Man, I'm looking forward to seeing you!"

18

When Hope picked up the phone, she sounded happy and well rested.

"Hi, Hope," Gene said, happy to hear her perked up.

"Good morning, Genie."

Gene told her, "I went out this morning, touring my past a little. You know, to find some powerful keys to our future. We need action, a little here and a little there, in our lives, every day, to make this change work."

"I'm glad to hear it, Gene. No worries here. Had a great chat with my mom about last night. She said, though she gives you a hard time sometimes, you're all right," Hope said, imitating Sylvie's voice. "She really is glad you are starting to find a way to feel better. So, you going to stay out?"

"Sweetie, yes—you'll never believe it, but I'm going to meet Pat Delaney, who worked in the AM Tower project."

"Really? Geez, Pat from back then? How'd you reconnect?" asked Hope.

"You know, it was minor. Or I thought it was minor. I found out from the guard at the tower, you know the big one, that Pat's still with the same company—and actually has moved up in the world. Along with my theme of moving from the past into the new future, I gave him a call on a lark. He's really jazzed to be meeting up with me, though. I guess you could say, 'It is time for men of action to unite, and we'll know what happens after that.' So how are you?"

"I *loved* last night. Oh, Jim being here, being happy, and bringing Dana, they filled the house with life, you know what I mean. We're the ecosystem, Genie, the family ecosystem, and as an ecologist I would say with some more cultivation, we could be on the path to restoration."

"That's funny, Hope. This morning I said we're a distributed electrical system. And I think I know what both of us mean," Gene said. "I think last night was the study hall we all needed. Now we need the practicum—I got convinced of that this morning. I really believe that I'm in a place where I can take on some changes. I just need guidance to find a regimen. I'm going to need to flip the right switches not just some days, but every day."

"I understand. I really know what you mean. I'm glad you're up and out; your thoughts run their way through your mind better that way. In fact, this morning I…"

Suddenly, Gene interjected, "Hey, listen to that!"

In wildlife observation, when someone says to listen, you don't say, "Listen to what?" as many untrained people would instinctively blurt out. You just listen. So Hope did.

It was silent for a moment on the line. The calls of the doves in the walnut trees began to descend from the branches and penetrate the phone's speaker.

At the Curtins' home, Hope could hear it: the sound making its way from the sacred ground of her family, her beloved trees and birds, to the new home they had created and were in the process of re-creating anew, lifestyle wise. Even through the phone, she instantly recognized the sounds. Jim's gift of the cell phone was already a tremendous boon to both of them. Jim really knew how to give. Hope kept listening.

A minute went by.

"Oh, Gene, thank you!" she finally said. "Have *such* a good day!"

"Maybe it can be…we'll see," he said. "Say, were you going to tell me something?"

Hope responded, "It's OK, I'll tell you later."

After hanging up, Hope deduced that Gene had yet to eat, and her giddiness over the stone still remained hers alone. Her morning had been magical, though she hadn't told Gene yet. Waiting to hear from Gene about the stone, she felt expectant. It hadn't been easy lately. *How nice it is to be looking forward to something exciting again,* she thought.

19

[Synesthesia is a state in which a sensation that normally occurs in one sense modality occurs when another modality is stimulated. It can take the form of seeing a sound, hearing a picture, smelling a color, or other forms. For example, one might taste that something is yellow, or hear the sound of cherry flavor. The cause and physiology of synesthesia in the brain is not completely understood. It can happen to the same person regularly, or it can happen suddenly to someone who has never experienced it before. On this day, Gene experienced synesthesia. This chapter is Gene's real-time, first-person report of his experience.]

The stream is really moving. Man, oh man, must be thousands of gallons of water flowing every minute, on their way past the point where I am standing here on the west side of the stream at Riverbank Park. I feel particularly observant of the river this morning. And I notice how observant I am, consciously. I even noticed the thought cross my mind about how, in physics experiments, observers alter the subjects through only their observation. I wonder where that thought came from.

The serenity of the water is drawing me lower down the bank, closer to the stream. I can hear the ripples in the water. I remember Rima said last night that beating vibrations from music had risen from her feet to fill the pain-wracked, all-but-dead zones of her physical body with a rhythmic energy that began to rejuvenate her life.

She must have had some remarkable kind of rejuvenation! She suffered in her youth so much, her body being so near to total defeat. And yet, real as I am, she was sitting there in complete gracefulness and gorgeousness last night.

While I am recalling Rima's rejuvenation story that began with rhythm, I want to ask her how visiting that nightclub and feeling some kind of energy rise up her body affected her life after that moment, day by day. What did she do the next day, and the next? She couldn't have visited the club every day. She needed her friend to even get there, and she hardly had the energy to be awake most hours of the day! Did she bring some elements from the club, like the type of music she heard there, and perhaps the nutritious drinks or something about the atmosphere, back into her apartment? And what did she bring back mentally, that she revisited in her mind and held on to when she needed a guiding light, in order to let herself be slowly changed and healed? What were her new commitments and her new choices?

Now I notice the rippling stream's lapping sounds—they are rhythmic. Thousands of gallons streaming by a minute—that makes for a complex beat! It sure transcends in complexity the beat of an electric metronome or alternating switch. But, by golly, in this moment, I can feel it. It is as though being close to the river is letting me be aware of new portals of information about nature and reality. I feel, out of nowhere, that I am being transformed from ordinary dimensions of consciousness into being in the presence of the sacred.

My head is being filled with the sound of the rushing and rippling stream, starting from my ears and flooding inward, backward, and forward. Now the sound is overflowing the confines and limits of my sense of hearing. The sensation is spilling over the banks of my auditory system. I know it is overflowing my auditory perception, but I wonder what it will flood into. What other systems of my perception are available to serve as the "floodplain," as it were, for all of this sound perception to spill into? And do I have a valve to control how much of this sensation floods from my hearing into my other senses, or will the sensation take me over beyond my say-so? I am a bit disoriented, slightly afraid of what is happening, yet to be so intimately taken into the river's vibration is like an embrace of love.

My whole head pulses, and I must descend from standing toward the ground. I am lowering my buttocks toward this pebbly riverbank. In this squat, gravity is working differently on my spine, hips, thighs, knees, ankles, *feet, and toes on both sides of my body, my prosthetic side just as much as my biological side. I trust my body completely in this squatting posture.*

Now the river's decadent pulsing rhythm has completely overrun my auditory system, and I am seeing the rhythm as a pattern of light, all around the river—under, on the surface, and above it. This is like nothing I have ever seen before. The river is completely glistening, luminescent, and pulsing visually to the rhythmic pattern that I am hearing.

The visual pattern is now beginning to change and move. I cannot describe it as a reflection of any light. It is not generated by any external light, even a light greater than the sun, even if all the great light shows in the world were happening here at once. No, it is a perception of a different quality.

What is happening is that the light pattern is changing in sync with the sound of the river changing. It is giving me chills as it shares information with me.

I know now that I am receiving a vision. Moments ago, I would have had no idea what that meant, but now I know I am being spoken to by an intelligence that surrounds this river, and I now suspect might surround all things. Information is being transmitted in each shape and pattern the light forms, just as certain as if a billboard were erected midriver with a sign that said, Follow the visual pattern. *All I am to do is witness.*

The light is golden. It is as wide as the river and now beginning to draw in from both banks. It is as long as the river's flow, and now it is beginning to draw inward to the very spot where I am. The light of the entire river, from bank to bank, from beginning to end, is being attracted in all four directions to the center of the river, straight out from where I am squatting.

The golden light penetrating in, under, and above the streaming waters is now becoming a cyclone, and I, the unsuspecting visionary, am becoming a hurricane tracker. What I can tell for sure is that I am to follow the light as it rotates, in rhythm, and set my attention to continue witnessing the very center of the vortex.

While it started with the vortex's axis spinning exactly at the center of the river, now the eye of this cyclone of light is beginning to tilt and drift away from the very center of the river, moving a little closer to me and a little further from me, a little to the left of me, upriver, and a little to the right, downriver.

I am the meteorologist of this pulsating system of light; that is all I know of what is happening, but I will keep tracking it. My attention is calm and light upon this wondrous sight, shifting organically, spinning furiously, slowly repositioning.

I am somehow certain the center of rotation is slowing further. It is beginning to stop about two-thirds of the way toward the eastern—or opposite—side of the steam from where I am standing. The place it is showing me is also slightly downstream from me. However, it is still in view. The slowing of the rotation is almost complete now.

I am hearing a communication now, saying, "Here. Location, here." And I know this is part of the vision's purpose. The light is still as bright and fast-spinning as before. Only its location is fixed.

Now the stream's overwhelming rhythm continues to pulse more strongly, until it is nearly a pounding, but still it is not painful. Hearing, seeing, and feeling this rhythm is a "pounding" in my head in the same way that a fresh rainfall sounds blissfully pounding on my new home's broad, safe, protective roof.

There is more communication coming. The light pattern is intensifying and more concentrated and smaller and tangible. It now looks as though it is made of physical material, as though it could hold something, should something precious be placed in it. If I had words for what I was seeing, I would point to this vision and call it a box of light. The light box is now sinking, as though it is a ship's hull gradually taking on water, going under the surface little by little. Its brilliant glow projects radially from the box as far outward as the river's banks and as high as my head as I squat. My attention is rapt with every ray of detail. The box is reinforcing itself now, with some of the radial rays of light "folding up" into the descending vessel. And still it sinks lower.

Now more of the light box is underwater than is abovewater. And in a moment...yes, now, it is completely submerged. I feel a longing for this box, like that for a loved one, as it slowly sinks. The box now shines a golden light that penetrates the water beneath the surface, while above the surface the glow has become too faint to see. Before, the subsurface river was unseeable, and now I see every minnow and stone in the river. Every piece of detritus, from walnut leaves to plastic bags floating down the river like jellyfish can be seen in high resolution. Also, now, as clearly as I see the shorebank, I see that at the point of the light, the river is as deep as I am tall when I stand. Down, down toward the bottom the light box is sinking, arriving on the river bottom. I sense a thud *as the light box lands, suggesting there is a physicality to its energy. I am receiving the signal that the light box has reached the place that I am meant to know about. And now, the light that illuminated the whole river has withdrawn. Only a box, no bigger than a crate that would sit on the river bottom, is illuminated.*

I sense the long surge of vibrational rhythm that overflowed into my visual system beginning to subside. The pulsing energy in the front and back of my head is exiting my skull through my ears. The vibration that draws me to squat facing toward the rhythm's source, the ground near the stream bank, is lessening in intensity. I am stretching my legs, rising from my unique set of feet through my legs and my spine, upright again.

I am most acutely aware that my blur of hearing and seeing, my synesthesia, which had given the sound of rippling water a second life as colors, is beginning to fade. My conventional perception is being restored. Once again, the sound of ripples is only heard, no longer miraculously "seen" as eerie light. At the same time, the light box deep under the river is becoming dimmer and harder to see, diminishing gradually.

The submerged vision of a box of light has faded to naught but a single, swirling candle-like apparition, positioned within a boxlike apparition that seems to be solidifying, but for lack of light, invisible. And now even the one, swirling "candle" underneath the river that flows swiftly and heavily by is extinguishing itself. It is gone.

I feel alive to the embodied dimension of vibrational frequency in a more electric way. I believe the effect of the impressions burned into my mind from this vision, whose occurrence I still cannot fully comprehend, will be deep in impact and lasting in duration.

20

For decades, ever since they'd started dating, Gene and Hope had considered Riverbank Park to be their special place. It was their family's vital connection to the elements and beauty of nature. Gene was intimately familiar with the vicinity. In his heart, he regarded the area with an esteem reserved for the sacred.

As familiar as his knowledge of the general Riverbank Park area was, Gene felt that he knew ten times as well the exact place under the river where the "light box" had sunk. It was burned into his memory. It was about thirty feet upstream from the footbridge (exactly half the distance of a pitcher from home plate, a metric he used for an estimate) and about fourteen feet into the stream from the east bank of the river—that day. Depending on the height of the river's crest on any given day, Gene knew that the distance to shore would vary. Gene determined that he would be making a special return visit to Riverbank Park's east shore in a short time.

Gene stood solidly on the earth at the riverbank, giving himself a moment for disbelief to transform into integration.

With a glance at his left wrist, Gene saw that if he left now, he would reach True Security at 10:00 a.m. Apparently, sudden onsets of synesthesia came with an impeccable sense of timing. Up the sloped bank and under the doves' nests he went.

Just before Gene got to his car, a loud popping sound came from the far end of his right leg, down where his prosthetic foot was attached. It startled Gene, who for an instant worried that he had gotten a crack in his prosthetic foot. But when he lifted his foot to get a closer look, a cracked walnut shell was revealed in his footprint.

"Still alive, still cracking!" he ribbed himself. "Hey, look at me… I'm balancing on one foot!"

A short drive later, Gene arrived, almost equally as curious to see the headquarters of True Security, Inc., as he was to reunite with Pat.

"Glad you could pop in on such short notice, Gene!" Pat said as he greeted him. "I'm just feeling enthusiastic about seeing you again, without any reason I can even pinpoint."

"I'd say I have an enthusiastic view on today, too," Gene said with a calm smile. "So let's see what happens."

They sat in the office of the senior manager of building security accounts. The suite was through a broad, clean door behind a warm reception area, on the second floor of a last-generation office building in the center of town. The office itself was painted in a black-and-white motif, with some exposed original red brick. Pat's office had windows facing in two directions, south and west, so that at ten o'clock in the morning, indirect sunlight was shining into the office.

Pat wore a blue tie, a tie clip with the True Security insignia, and black slacks, and had a shiny, large-faced watch on his left wrist. Gene was in his morning sweats and windbreaker.

"So, Gene, I'm dying to know: what on Earth prompted you to call me this morning? Actually, first, how did you even know where to find me?"

"Thank Brian," Gene said, hinting.

"You dog, you! You went back to the old building; well, it was new then," exclaimed the man in the tie.

"We are a little like that building," Gene joked.

"Ain't that the truth?" Pat laughed. "I'm no new building like I was when I was at AM. That was my first gig, you know."

"Is that right. Well, you've made an impression on Brian in your creaky agedness; at least, that's the sense that I got from him."

"Oh?" Pat asked.

Gene assured him it was true, relating, "He spoke of you with respect and said, 'I think Mr. Delaney would be happy to talk with you.'"

"Absolutely true, I am; there's something about you that's just bringing new life in here this morning, man!" Pat exclaimed.

"You don't know how good it is to hear that, Pat. You really don't."

"Try me, Gene. What wouldn't I understand?"

"I just haven't been at my most vital. My edge got dull, you know? You could say my footing slipped."

"I'm listening, man. Vitality, sharp focus, and footing. You gotta believe those are things I make sure that my guards—and everyone in my department—keep among their priorities," Pat said. "Maybe in different words, but I know exactly what you mean."

"Well, in the past two weeks, and especially the past twenty-four hours, I was able to get reinvigorated, connect with my wife in a whole new way, exemplify being a better man to my son, stop reliving my former accomplishments as the highest I'll ever reach in life, and actually feel inspired about the future," Gene declared, surprising even himself.

"Bro, that's awesome!" Pat said.

"You're right. It is. If I told you what it took to get here…"

"Tr—"

"I know: 'Try me.' We'll cross that bridge when we come to it. I promise you, man to man," Gene said. "But what about you? You caught some breaks, eh?"

"Tell you what, I guarded every building from AM onward with all my capability, every day. I had the best rating in everything measured in the industry, from crime prevention to courteousness, through six different assignments. After AM, it was the Woolton building, then the Country Spring Mall. Then I had, um, what was next? Oh, yes, the Nightshade Dance Club, the Best Friend Kennel and Animal Training Center, and the playground and high-powered play fountain at Riverbank Park for the city. That's the one wh—"

"Interesting," Gene interjected. "That last one. I never saw you there at the park. And I would have, I think. Not many months went by without me going there with the family."

"That's the thing I'm telling you about, bro, the one that changed just about everything. There was this one kid who came to the playground in a wheelchair, helped by an aide. He got to be in the playground with the other kids, but his playing, obviously, it was different. No climbing up the jungle gym for him; no, just wheeling around the perimeter by himself or with kids who were either bored, catching their breath, on "time out," or unpopular at the time. I'll tell you, Gene, on my first day, when I saw him, I noticed that not only was he different from the other kids, but he was different from other kids I had seen in wheelchairs. An adventurous and bright disposition this kid had, when he would arrive at the park…

"After about forty-five minutes, this kid went into what looked like a seizure. His face looked really agonized for like fifteen seconds, though no sounds were coming out of him. He recovered, but then he was just droopy and dim-eyed. I had no idea whether this was routine for him or not. And as he was already in a chair, it wasn't clear to me whether anyone else—kid, aide, or other adult—noticed what happened. I kept my focus as a security guard, thinking my job was to promote a crime-free environment, not to play medic, but I had a full view of what had happened, and it left me feeling really bad for this kid.

"My second day, I couldn't believe it. Same thing: he comes to play, the new day seeming to have revived him, and just over halfway into it, boom!—a dramatic seizure and a drugged-looking recovery. It must have just sucked. It didn't help his popularity, either. And that helpless kid…my God.

"The third day, I was watching this kid like an eagle. One game he can play sitting in a chair is a kind of gambling that he and the other kids do with quarters. Double heads or double tails, and the second kid who flips the coin wins the other kid's quarter. The kids played it with stealth, knowing they weren't supposed to be doing it. I notice that he wins twice before rolling to the bathroom. Underneath the overhang of the playground bathrooms, there's a vending machine for soda. Two coins in, one soda can out. He's fast; I'm not sure anyone else saw it. The kid drinks it halfway behind the wall, where he's shielded from view, and then rolls back to the play structure. Bang—seizure!

"Look, that day, I wasn't a parent-guardian, nor a doctor, nor an expert. I just saw what my eyes saw. I can understand it totally, man: a kid with a disability just wants to have some fun and make some mischief like the other kids who can run and play pranks. Honestly, I didn't know what to do. I ran through some scenarios in my mind. I could tell the aide, who could either accept or reject what I told her. If she accepted it, sure, I might get thanked for noticing the problem, but I could also possibly be the one who kept the kid from being brought out to the park and to the playground. Not an easy choice for me.

"Instead, I could tell the city what I saw. I know there's money in the deal, though, both for the city and the vending machine company. There was cash on the line between the city and True Security as well, for that matter. What could an anecdotal eyewitness prove, anyway, to a health and recreation department? Rocking the boat might get me in trouble with some players above my pay grade at the time.

"That's why I didn't tell True Security, either, to be honest. Risky for a guard to opinionate too much…

"So here's what I did, Gene. I started an anonymous campaign through the Letters to the Editor in the *Post*, stating that a solution was needed to a problem in our community indicated by the fact that 'some passersby and concerned adults' in Riverbank Park had been noticing that 'certain children' were experiencing 'various symptoms' after ingesting 'a variety of processed food products' from the vending machine in the playground area.

"Well, this gathered a lot of support in the community in a rather short period of time. By a couple of weeks later, the number of supportive statements sent into the *Post* equaled forty-five to fifty percent of the number of households in the municipal area who were in communication with the local paper. The most popular solution mailed in from the public, by far, was to have the processed food and drinks in the Riverbank Park playground replaced with untained healthy food and drinks. It was overwhelming, really," Pat said with a bit of awe in his voice.

"I think I remember something about this, Pat," Gene said. "I have to tell you, I was in the other fifty percent. I was just too busy with pushing the electricity business and raising my family to really pay attention to food and health. But I'm incredibly interested in hearing your story."

"I'm not surprised, to be honest with you. But it's all good. The support was overwhelming, with the majority of even the other half of town not opposed to the campaign, just not focusing on it," Pat reassured him.

Then he continued, "It got to where the city council was having an epidemiologist consider the economic, social, and health impacts of the available foods and beverages in the park, and moving in the direction of passing a resolution on the vending machine.

"At that point, there grew a call for the originator of this 'anonymous movement' to be revealed; they wanted to have a hero! The way it panned out was a citizen journalist took up a beat at the park playground, and three days later, the story broke. It said that there was only one adult who spent enough time at the Riverbank Park playground to observe the effects that were being reported, while also being unemotional enough about it to keep the campaign anonymous, and that that person, the investigative page-five article implied, was 'a vigilant yet stoic security guard employed by True Security.' Also known as...me.

"I'd been observing the politics generated by this campaign, and the very strong community support encouraged me to think that soon would be the time to come out and let the whole truth be known. If True Security was going to have me canned under the scrutiny of the whole town for defending the health of the next generation, bring it on.

"Two days later, a horde of photographers and reporters camped in the park near the playground. The CEO of True Security was there, too, trying to get interviewed to control the media narrative. The press now knew everything about me. Whether or not they followed me home, I'm not sure, but my address was made public at that point, which meant that I, as a security professional, was going to have to relocate.

"If I let this go any longer, it might have gotten out of hand. So I fessed up."

"Dang! And now you're here in this chair. What the hell happened after you fessed to starting the initiative?" Gene asked.

"In the end it was the best outcome I could have hoped for," Pat replied. "I felt safe in this community and showered with appreciation simply for being an ally of children. It was its members who protected my job, my name, my ability to get housing with privacy. Mothers, fathers, teachers, real-estate agents: they all kept their alliance for healthier children, through healthier vending machines, intact to let the city know there would be protests if anything happened to hamper me or to harm True Security's name, as long as True Security respected me and kept advancing my career here. In fact, any politician or city administrator who used True Security in the years following got a popularity boost.

"To this day, as senior manager of building security accounts, I have a different set of criteria than any other security firm before us. It's all about whether or not the institution who wants our services is truly safeguarding the health of the people and the land. We're not going into situations where the client isn't working with us to create a safe space for well-being," Pat said, finishing up his story.

Then he added, "So what about you? You looked pretty engrossed while I was telling you this story, man. What gives?"

Gene just sat there with his mouth agape.

21

Amazed at what he'd just heard, Gene checked the wall calendar to make sure it was still the year he thought it was. The possibility that this was another lifetime, or suddenly another world, seemed equally likely. *First this morning's teleportation into a dimension where a river speaks through visual messages of light*, he thought, *and now, as if that wasn't enough…Where was this guy sent from? Pat's concern for people's nutrition, health, and well-being, which, through one turn or another, might have gotten him and his company in hot water, instead got him promoted within his firm, thanks to his popularity with the public?*

Security Unit 10 was one of more than three dozen units that True Security was able to deploy to meet different clients' needs. Security Unit 10 was the specialized unit equipped for providing security at events near bodies of water. It possessed a number of supplies that augmented its security guards with the ability to become first-responder rescuers. Not all security firms provide rescuing capabilities, but True Security had implemented the idea in the past few years. The idea of rescuing people had been brought up in a meeting one day by Pat Delaney, who had said, "Look, we all like to think that security is preventive—and it is. But with the uncertain state of the world today, how much safer would you feel knowing that the people who are meant to be keeping you safe also have a plan in case anything goes downhill? We all know that feeling, and the public definitely does."

After that meeting, True Security developed a water rescue-capable deployable unit. This idea was a hit in the community, which loved its riverside recreation.

For Pat, the realization that every once in a while, security providers have got to reach out and help somebody came as he reflected on the playground vending machine incident years later. Internally, he came to the conclusion that it is human hubris that would suggest security can keep people healthy and safe without sometimes needing to lend a helping hand to those who have fallen into danger.

Pat figured, "It's not like healthy food in children's areas is a new idea. It's just that this kid—you know, I never told anyone his name; I *so* wouldn't want to embarrass him, ever—this kid made me see that we human beings are a constantly improving species. So the playground didn't have it quite right. That's simply the way of the world—we haven't got it all the way right yet. This goes for healthy, safe communities and just about any other aspect of life; we're always a work in progress. We are inching toward taking responsibility—all around our homes, all around town, all around the nation, all around the globe. I can't rescue the world, but maybe one corner of the world or one person in it.

"Now, tell me—and remember, I'm 'vigilant' so you can't put much by me," Pat chuckled. "Why do I get the feeling this is so darned important to you personally?"

Gene related to Pat his hopes for his retirement and new home, juxtapositioned with his accident and his diagnosis of diabetes. He informed Pat about Rima and Don, and what Jim, and now Dana, had brought into his life. Gene transparently shared, having left behind much of his earlier reservation, his new passion that he and Hope had for each other and each other's well-being, and even spoke in detail about the river that morning. Well before Gene finished the full bit, Pat's eyes were wet with emotion and so wide open that a bright hue of white shone from his sclera.

"Gene," Pat said with a tremor in his voice, filled with an excited and firm determination, but with a respect for Gene's boundaries, "I want you to consider what you have to share."

"In what way, 'share'?" Gene asked.

"What you have experienced is precious. It's the inheritance we need to pass on to protect the safety and health of our young people and, in many socioeconomic ways, the nation."

Gene was catching on to Pat's point. "Pat, I've been bringing lights to people, not inspiration or spoken words," he demurred. "People's business is people's business."

"Yes and no, now, fella. Look at what I do. Professionally, I make other people's business my business, when a line is crossed and they are in need of an advocate, so they can ultimately advocate for themselves. Never does True Security take a position in interpersonal dramas that may be happening in public, and never do we enter the revenge business when someone says they've been pushed or shoved, literally or figuratively. True Security is all about advocating, moment by moment, for the decency, dignity, sovereignty, well-being, and life itself of the people we provide security for. I know you feel me on this—that's why your jaw is slack again, bro! You feel it when I talk about taking a stand and being an advocate for making a difference in people's lives, because you know you've experienced being on the receiving end of it—and richly at that, I might add."

Gene paused, inhaled, and sighed deeply, letting this sink in.

In the silence of the room, the most recently spoken words reverberated off the brick. Cars went by. Smoke rose from the chimney on the roof across the street. Then, over Pat's right shoulder, Gene saw a dove land on the windowsill. The dove sounded its low cooing, adding a rich, warm reminder of his loved ones to the moment's pregnant stillness.

Pat bluntly asked, "So, do you wanna share? Here's a possibility: I have a high school assembly I am speaking at at three o'clock. The youths' ears and minds are so hungry, brother!"

Hungry.

"Good point, Pat. It's forty-five minutes after noon now. I'm going to take a lunch break and think about it," Gene said, suddenly noticing his appetite as he began to rise and turn in his chair.

"Oh, and which high school?" he asked, tacitly accepting Pat's invitation.

Section 3:
The Secrets of the Seven
Sacred Stones

22

Between the shade that covered the Corvair and Gene's travel cooler, the glassware and the food itself were still a refreshing temperature, ready to be enjoyed. Gene's first bite of the food tasted marvelous and beyond that, capped a morning of incredible receiving of gifts, people, and even *visions*.

As Gene used his fork to mix the vegetables and the sauce, he heard the unexpected ting of glass on metal. With the next forkful, a mysterious box appeared.

Knowing Hope could be tacky yet creative enough to pack a box within a box, Gene thought a long *Oookaaayyy…what's this about?*

He opened the box. Now it was Gene's turn to behold the curves and carvings and have his palm and fingers caress this most meaningful of minerals. Given his time at the river that morning, he associated this stone's round edges with the effect that stones undergo when ground for aeons in currents of water. Where had Hope gotten this stone from? Had she somehow made it? In any case, Gene felt affection toward Hope for letting him discover the stone in such a surprising yet appropriate way.

With too many mysteries to solve all at once, Gene decided to focus on comprehending what the stone actually said. Holding the stone, which gave a new meaning to "precious mineral," at arm's length, Gene read:

FOOD, WATER, AND AIR FOR LIFE FORCE

That minimalist message sure seemed to fit with what Gene been experiencing that day: walking in the crisp early morning air, soaking in the fresh river water's rhythm, and eating the first of his and Hope's new kind of healthy meal for lunch that was nutritious, hydrating, and life-affirming.

23

Gene savored what was possibly the most exceptional bagged lunch of his adult life while digesting what was clearly the most extraordinary morning of his postaccident phase. In stark contrast to the afternoon slumps that he had experienced for years, Gene felt nourished and noticed a vivacious energy rising in his body after lunch. *Very uncommon*, he thought. *I'm getting out of this car and I'm going to cover some ground!*

Gene yearned for his body to be whole again, deep down, and he was finding sensation to be his doorway into feeling somatically integrated. The spark that kicked in enabled him to feel both of his legs with much richer anatomical sensation, almost fiber by fiber. His sensory nervous system was aware of the web of fasciatic connective tissue extending from his Achilles upward through the IT bands up the outside edges of his legs to their pelvic insertion ligaments. From this greater sensation reemerged Gene's capability to tread with a bit of purpose and pace down the sidewalk, passing shops and bars.

He remembered the severe physical limitations that Rima had overcome when she had felt rhythm cause movement to pulse through her body. As this confident, gliding, and accelerating walk took hold of Gene, he explored new streets, and he experienced his own proprioception (the nervous system's awareness of its own movements and positioning). Finding that his body was capable of more than he had believed, his sinews stretched and his ligaments gently groaned. What had been solid endpoints to Gene's ranges of motion in his ankles, hips, hamstrings, psoas, spine, shoulders, wrists, and neck began to melt into traversable passes. His bodily sensations felt like the liquefaction of mountains, which he had seen in footage of landslides. There was flowing earth where there had been rigidness. He was alive and feeling again where he had been deadened and numbed.

As much as he loved the bodily thawing he was feeling, Gene was also playing a game in his mind. He had discovered that, all at the same time, his animated awareness was playing both aikido and poker with the still-present limp that was apparent as he stepped on his surgically enhanced foot. The banter in these games went, basically, like this: *OK, body, you're handing me an asymmetrical frame? Well, I see your limp and raise you a strut.*

And strut he did. For the first time since donning his prosthesis, Gene leveraged in and leaned forward, far past the "idling speed" on the throttle of his mobile capacities.

Past the barber shop, the creamery, the windows of the art gallery, Gene was trotting. He sailed around the corner of First Avenue onto Main Street and then saw the hardware store. Yes, *the* one. The last place he had been before getting into his car and driving his way to within a fraction of a breath of his demise.

And yet, here he was, more full of deep and powerful breath than he had been at any time since well before that day. The saying, *the night is coldest just before the sunrise*, occurred to Gene.

He stopped power walking but kept the ambulation rhythm in his knees, in his pumping shoulders and fists. His face remained the face of a man in the zone. He had remembered the paint and tiling on the storefront as being drabber. though he understood that psychologically, he may well have created dark clouds around his memory of the location. He took in the scene exactly as it was, celebrating the vibrancy and sharpness of the colors, the red and yellow of the hardware shop logo. Had the fateful day truly been as hazy as he remembered it, or was that his hazier mind of the past? Today he was a mental martial artist with consciousness of his body, as well as a flexing power walker reclaiming his physical vigor and grace.

To reaffirm his physicality, Gene had an urge to *ground, and* facing the spot his car had been parked on that fateful day, he allowed himself to fold forward at the hips. He swan dove into the full curvature of his spine, arms tumbling like waterfalls toward the ground. As his fingertips and his gaze came closest to the concrete, an oblong yet roughly pie-shaped stone came into focus, a glint of sunshine reflecting off of it. Chiseled into it were letters.

Stepping his left foot about eighteen inches further left to widen his stance, he assumed a lunge with his lower body, torso, and nose directly aligned toward this stone. The letters were slightly occluded by a patina; torquing his hips leftward to reach his right arm for the stone, he tapped the side of the stone with his index finger. Some of the patina crumbled into powder within the grooves of the letters. Taking the stone up with a fingertip grip, Gene's right hand turned the engraved side down, and much of the powdery crust fell out. Regripping the stone in his palm, he turned it toward his eyes as he simultaneously exhaled, stabilized his core, and pressed his grounded legs to rise powerfully out from his lunge.

PHYSICAL AND MENTAL EXERCISE, read the stone.

Amen to that, Gene thought with a rejuvenating inhale. *Amen to tha—oh, the school assembly!*

24

The energetic crowd buzzed with chat of all kinds. The teens had heard of Pat Delaney, who at five minutes after three o'clock, had been well introduced. Hundreds of teens sat at attention as Pat ascended three stairs onto the riser set at one end of the gymnasium under a basketball net that had been raised to the ceiling. Stately championship banners hung from the rafters above him, prizes dating from the '50s to recent years, representing the heritage of the teens who had passed through the halls of Middletown High School.

Pat began by saying how fortunate he felt to again be given an opportunity to share his story.

"The last time I spoke here, those who are seniors today were sophomores, and many of you here today may not have been at Middletown High School at all. It is a blessing to be able to share my story, because what happened to me was seen as it happened by many of your parents. I hope that, when they read the papers and the interviews, it inspired something in them. I hope that in some way, what has happened in my life has made being responsible and caring a little more doable for people in this town. And I believe it has, because you are here today, and everything I hear from Principal Jake is that every class that comes through this school is more impressive as young men and women than the last.

"Before the assembly, I know your teacher probably told you the basics of my story, and you got to discuss it. I am grateful for what happened, even though I was nervous at first about what would happen to me if I spoke up for the cause. However, in this assembly, as compared to the one two years ago, I'm hoping to bring some new energy in for you all. It kinda depends on whether someone shows up…

"This morning—truly, five hours ago—I was greeted by a man I had last seen before I even had the security job at Riverbank Park. I used to see him at the job I had at the AM Tower, early in the morning. He would shake my hand or say, 'Hello; good morning,' before entering the building to do his job. His job was electrical contracting. His company put the lights in the AM Tower you see on the town's skyline to this day. Also, if you visit Riverbank Park in the late fall and winter and see the city's holiday lights, that is his work. And I know it means a lot to Mr. Gene Curtin that I'm telling you this, because he put a lot of passion and hard work into beautifying his town with the 'electrifying' skills he has been given.

"Today, Gene found me by getting my card from a security guard who currently works for me at True Security at the AM Tower. Of course, when Gene asked me how I got here, I told him my story. He looked at me with such captivation, I was curious what was going through his mind.

"Then Gene told me he had the rudest awakening of his life not very long ago, still recently enough to be raw, in which he flipped his car on Main Street. The accident nearly injured some children. Medics found Gene trapped under the wreckage, unconscious in a hypoglycemic coma. After days in the hospital, nurses determined that his foot was suffering from neuropathy and infection and had to be amputated. You might have also seen this terrifying incident in the news.

"Now, some of you might think this man and I would be opposites, me famous for caring for kids' health and safety, and Gene the guy who nearly walloped kids with a fast-moving metal object he was no longer capable of being responsible for," Pat said to laughs from the audience.

"But no, we came together this morning. Gene and his wife, Hope, and their son, Jim, who's just a little older than you and is a college student, are all becoming warriors, protectors, and advocates for health, starting in their own home. They are discovering the best ways to advocate for their birthrights of nourishment and practices that let their bodies function up to their full potential. Inspired by a neighbor who told them he once had diabetes and then recovered, they've gone into study mode and come up with really valuable discoveries. Gene's going to tell you about what he's discovered, three principles he shared with me. Why he's still searching for effective whole-health practices. Why he is never finished learning and is increasingly committed to giving back to others. So, if he's here, which to be honest I don't know, I present my new and old friend, Gene Curtin!"

Gene entered the gym. He had been listening from within earshot just outside. Not sure whether he'd go in, he'd felt what Pat was saying. Neither his upper lip, which quivered, nor his arm, which opened the door, nor his legs, which strode into the gymnasium, would stay still. The students' applause and occasional cheers rumbled in his heart as he crossed midcourt feeling strong yet showing the hitch in his step. Reaching the riser, he walked up the steps and he felt his surgical wound pounding in his foot, and paused there at the top step. Pat moved toward him, hugged him, and walked him toward the podium under the lights, in front of five hundred students and forty-nine teachers. After a beat, Pat took a half step back from the podium and allowed attention to shift to Gene. With the student body fixing their attention on him, Gene unhooked the second microphone from the podium and held it as he moseyed a few shuffling steps toward the front of the riser.

With a little effort, Gene sat down with his feet dangling over the edge of the riser and began to untie his shoe. Then he began to speak deliberately and slowly.

"I want to thank my son, Jim, who attended school here a couple of years ago, who you all remind me of; my wife, who dedicated herself to understanding life and has helped me expand my worldview immeasurably while she herself has kept learning; my mother in law, Sylvie, who cares even though she has difficulty expressing it, and my friend Pat Delaney." The crowd cheered enthusiastically in appreciation.

"I would not be here today if not for them. Not here in this gym, not having the privilege to meet you here at the assembly today, and quite possibly not alive. I had surgery to remove part of my foot from my body, my flesh from my flesh. The truth is, now I know I am fortunate the amputation didn't have to be worse, lucky indeed considering my ignorance and habits before that time.

"Here is a key point: it was love, my family around me, that drew me to awaken from the general anesthesia.

"And again after being discharged and prescribed toxic medications, when I was depressed and demolished about losing my mobility and other capacities—dang it, just as we were supposed to be celebrating our retirement, the freedom I had worked hard for all my life—my wife, Hope, was there to let me fall down in her arms, hit the bottom, and literally and figuratively stand back up.

"When the task of interpreting the diabetes dietary advice seemed like too much to bear, Hope and Jim brought love into the process and helped me learn to eat the food—leaves, seeds, nuts, fruits, roots, flowers, sprouts, and sea vegetables—that gives us nutrients and promotes good health. I've changed, and I've begun to enjoy giving myself foods with whole nutrition that my body can absorb and use for its metabolism in an efficient way, just like a tree needs to grow in good, fertile soil. Life wants to live where clean air and water circulate with energizing nutrients, and take away our toxins daily. Further, I know that, thanks to my family, I am starting to eat foods that flip the healthy switches in my body's system.

"I will describe to you my three principles. They've come to me so recently, and they probably would have never come if I weren't intensely reflecting on how to rejuvenate my health. You're the first, besides Mr. Delaney, to hear these principles, because, as Pat knows, they only became clear to me this morning during a walk on the west side of Riverfront Park.

"One: cellular replacement. Did you know the human body is constantly replacing old cells with new ones? What we do in our lifestyles has a significant impact on how these new cells will regenerate. We're feeding our genes. And I'm not just saying that because of my name!"

The biology teacher and teachers' pets got the joke, at first, then others.

"Two: body consciousness. You ever hear an adult or teacher, or even a friend, say you might want to be less judgmental? Frankly, in high school, I didn't even know what that meant. Wasn't judging what we just do all the time? Well, it's like this: our body is perhaps the least judgmental being you'll ever be in relationship with. It believes us if we want to be healthy, and believes us if we don't care, and responds accordingly. Largely, it does for us as we do to it. Bottom line: it is us who creates the outcomes that we want. The body does what it does with what it is given in food, exercise, activity, our thoughts, and our spirits. Its responses don't lie, and its outcomes are usually predictable.

"Three: perpetual motion on the whole-health spectrum. Here in this gymnasium, some legends have played. But they'll tell you, no matter how good they got and how much they improved their game, there was always somebody better. There have been some benchwarmers on these teams, too—necessary, of course, as backups and substitutes. No matter how the subs let their skills deteriorate, there was always somebody who had less skill than them. Our health is that way, too. Everyone—absolutely everyone—is in flux along a spectrum from bodily degeneration to radiant health, with skills, habits, and knowledge corresponding to their trajectory across that spectrum.

"I gotta tell you all something else. You might hardly believe me. That intensely reflective state I was in this morning continued long enough for me to realize that I still have yet to clear my destructive patterns, but I notice them, which is huge! And I have the readiness and an embodied foundation of interest in practices that can help me live a lifestyle I want. A lifestyle where all three of these principles are lived every day.

"In fact, coming to this assembly is only one stop among many for today, because I notice my patterns and I know I need to get more settled into live-affirming lifestyle practices. It's going to take positive habit formation over time—there's no substitute for that—and it's also going to involve one more thing immediately. This is something I will be doing this afternoon."

This statement made Pat raise his arms in a wide shrug. He stepped back to the podium and on its remaining mic, he interjected, "Oh, really?"

Gene's ignoring of Pat's interruption only added to the drama and curiosity in the gymnasium.

Gene slid off his untied right loafer. He then folded down his sock and slipped it off. Placing sock next to shoe, Gene unsecured the prosthesis, the two-thirds of his foot that was composite molding material, removed it from his biological foot as if he was breaking bread, and held it up above his shoulder.

The gymnasium gasped, and a moistness came into Gene's eyes, a spirited tremble to his voice, as he continued speaking.

"Here it is. Here is what happens if you address your lifestyle and diet too late," Gene told the teachers, school workers, and hundreds of youths with self-reproach. Remembering the family-room study, he continued, "Don't make your health a sideshow to anything—not to your career, not to the technological modernization of the economy, not to your social life, and not to your family life. A healthy body, a healthy nervous system and brain, a healthy expression of your genome—these parts of your phenotype--which you have a large amount of control over--are irreplaceable for your long-term happiness, and in fact, are fundamental to your being there for your future families, as well as to giving your best to your professions."

Gene dug deep inside himself for his final guidance, homespun and ineloquent as it might be.

"Definitely, definitely pursue your career aspirations, hang out with people and communities that fire your imagination, and if you desire, passionately raise that family you may want to have one day. I know your hearts will be drawn to all these things, and that's part of living. Still, remember to keep a smart eye on your lifestyle. Your body truly needs you."

Gene closed his speech with emphasis: "Young people, there isn't any amount of money in the universe that could have brought back those kids if my car had disastrously hit them. And no retirement account can bring my original foot back. That's what I've been taught. Go far in life, wherever your unique paths take you. Just take the three principles with you: cellular replacement, body consciousness, and the perpetual movement on the whole-health continuum.

"I leave you with that."

25

The gym-rumbling applause for Gene and Pat had lasted uncomfortably long for both men, and it continued even as they made their way to the exit and stood outside the gymnasium at Middletown High School. They certainly were grateful for the acknowledgment from the students. Where they stood talking just outside the gym's doors, the foundation of the old school building—a slab of cement that wrapped around the gymnasium—met the earth of the schoolyard. Patches of grass and rocky dirt surrounded them. One hundred feet or so to the west, the grass became the well-tended turf of the adjacent soccer field. Pat was standing on a patch of grass within a short distance of Gene, who was standing on the gym's concrete foundation.

A high school boy, perhaps an upperclassman, approached Pat and Gene from around the side of the gymnasium. His walk was the slightest bit awkward, less of a limp than an asymmetrical gait. Like many boys still coming off a growth spurt, still getting used to their gangly bodies, his feet would occasionally get caught beneath him. One foot would drag for a moment, catch the ground, and cause a cascade of pebbles, rocks, and puffs of dirt to precede him in the direction he was walking.

When the lad got near, his height became truly apparent. He looked humbly and sincerely at Pat for a moment and then simply said, "Thanks for what you did. I'm Perlis Huron. I have never met you face-to-face before. I owe you one."

Pat's eyes, as he recalled the name, bulged slightly out of their sockets as he failed to conceal his shock. He knew who this growing young man was. Pat's glance toward Gene conveyed exactly who Perlis Huron was. Then Gene realized it, too.

"What do you mean, Perlis?" Pat asked. "I see that you've come a long way physically. But what do you believe that you owe me?"

Perlis took a breath, looked down at his sneakered feet, looked up at the windows of the school, and began to speak. "I might not be here if it hadn't been for you. My story is a little incredible, even though it is a true story. What I now understand is that, through my body's seizures, I was a canary in a coal mine, responding to the excitotoxins in soft drinks. I suffered for days, going into seizures, as you witnessed. Did you know why I was in a wheelchair in the first place? I had been having seizures since I was three. I could walk just fine—most of the time—but sometimes the injuries caused by the seizures were so bad, my parents feared me walking unsupported. They and my doctors agreed it might be safest for me to be in a wheelchair so that when a seizure hit, I would be protected from sharp things that could puncture me, staircases I could fall down, etcetera; you get the idea.

"My parents had started me on sodas young. People might have known, or had a hint, that their excitotoxins disturbed my brain in such a way that happened, for me, to cause seizures—I sure noticed the pattern—but no one believed I could truly avoid this cycle, and I figured I'd have seizures my whole life.

"As a child, I liked risky, daredevil stuff. I liked to gamble. For me, it was fun and innocent—I just wanted to see if I could buy the can of soda without the adults noticing—and see what would happen if I got caught. The attention I got, plus the exceptions from having my homework due on time because of the seizures, didn't hurt, either. I thought I was getting ahead of the game, escaping from hard work and hard lessons.

"After years of goofing around like this, you came into my life on that fateful day when the playground became a hotbed of press and media types. You foiled my fun, messed with my plan. All of a sudden, where was my attention? To be honest, I saw you as competition for attention-king of the park. For quite a few years, I didn't understand why you became such a hero. Man, you were the big man in town! Only when I grew more understanding did I even ask about the *kind* and *quality* of attention each of us was getting, and for what reasons? And that's where the story gets more interesting...

"One day, I found a strange stone near one of the goalposts on the football field—I was allowed to play on wide-open grass fields—with carvings on it. How it got there was actually a bigger mystery to me than your identity ever was to the newspaper and this community. I guess that's because rocks can't write letters to the editor and get everyone trying solve the mystery. No, this carved stone was mine alone. I kept it that way, playing a game with myself to see how long I could keep the secret and come up with theories for its origin and meaning.

"It might sound funny, but from the day I found this stone, it became for me a token that symbolized an ideal of stability, strength, and patience. Not that I had those words for it at the time. It was just a stone that showed up and never wavered, whereas I had episode after episode, again and again in a crazy cycle, when I could not control my head and body's movements. What made it a special possession for me, one that I felt was like a refuge of peace within chaos, was the stone itself, its solid, cool feel, combined with what it said."

"Oh, yeah? What did it say?" Pat asked, while Gene continued standing here, wondering the same thing.

"It said 'A Quiet Mind.' At first I thought, *That's a sure way to get tongue-tied with a girl—or fail my math or history test. No, I don't ever want my mind to go quiet or blank.*"

"I can understand that," Gene interjected. "I've known the feeling. Always gotta know the next move and control the outcome..."

Pat nodded and Perlis smiled with appreciation. Then he continued, "So I put the stone in my underwear drawer, until one day, a substitute teacher who I only had for one day, the day before a test in history, said something that made sense to me. He asked us, all the students in the class, to really consider how many of the Cs, Ds, and Fs in the class could have been As and Bs if our patterns of thinking, saying, or doing, as if on autopilot, weren't making us act in certain ways?

"He said, for example, we could have formed a habit of not studying well during a period when one's family was going through a hard, stressful time. Even though those tough times may have passed, that behavior—not studying with an effective strategy—may have stuck with us from the past stress.

"The key to success in this grade, regardless of your past results in any previous grade, he said, is being adaptive to what's happening in the moment by getting the past *out* of our minds and into our wisdom experience. He asked us to consider how many times we had put our foot in our mouth, or showed up clueless to the test, or otherwise made a fool of ourselves, not fundamentally because of knowledge we lacked, but because our minds were filled to the brim with repeating loops and programs from the past that we had automatically inserted into our present. People often say and do things because their minds are cluttered with grievances, jealousy, anger, hurt. Do these patterns leave any attention actually free to meet the world as it is?

"Let me give you another example. I might make fun of a girl—you know, give her a rough time—who I actually liked, just because somewhere in my subconscious I was still reacting to another girl who had poked fun at or humiliated me. The girl I liked had nothing to do with that, except in my mind's stimulus response. That stimulus response is what serves us to quiet down. Then we go from 'talking to a girl equals defending myself from humiliation,' to 'let's see what arises if I feel this moment in the presence of myself and she.' We also go from 'a test tomorrow equals stress overload' to 'if I look at the class materials, how *can* I prepare for the likely questions the test will ask me?' It's a whole different experience.

"We can learn a lot from an antelope. An antelope's fear and trauma from being chased by a lion is in its body, and after the chase the antelopes can be seen physically shaking the immediate discomfort out of their bodies, not dwelling on the horrible thing that happened. That made sense for me, loving risky games and all. I practiced feeling the neural disturbances before a seizure happened. I started noticing mental trauma more often and always moving it down and out into my body out of my mind, knowing the mind tended to overload and short circuit. In my body, I would preempt seizures by shaking off my pain, abandonment, vengeance against my competitors, and so on, like a great wild antelope. Then I would be clear in the mind and also a bit wiser, abiding on a deeper level."

Perlis continued, "The night after the history class when I first heard these ideas, I slept at home as usual. When I went to get dressed the next morning, my underwear drawer happened to be nearly empty, and I caught a glimpse of the stone in the back of the drawer, the same one I'd picked up off the football field and put in the back of my drawer years prior. Just like it always had, it said 'A Quiet Mind,' and this time, I got it: I understood the inscription. Somehow, in that moment, there was a space for remembering how some guy—it turned out to be a security guard—had messed with my soda-seizure 'sick leave' game. That game had become repetitive, a habit. The allure of the habit, and what I got out of it as a so-called reward—people's temporary sympathetic attention, at least for a while—became stronger than my even asking myself, 'Do I truly want seizures?' And I forgave you. Fate had brought us together in this world, you teaching me something without trying to be a teacher, but just by being in the flow of what was a core value for you: defending security, safety, and well-being. I realized that a core value is a like a stone, having stability that endures through the storm. With my constantly chattering mind and habitual games, suddenly I saw you as a kind of Jedi, who quieted his mind so that he could rest upon and live in core values—like health, safety, and security, and probably others, as well.

"Finally, after getting this point, the community's celebration of what you did and who you were made sense to me, maybe in a special way that most of the community hadn't even appreciated, because the exact complementary qualities that balanced and altered my life forever were found in you and, at long last, transferred to me.

"You see, thanks to quieting my mind of all its games that didn't serve me, I've eaten like a champ since my freshman year. First my seizures stopped, and that was a major achievement. Plus, the old injuries I sustained as a young child—puncture wounds and the like from flailing about—began to heal. I'm a climber, a wrestler, and a swimmer now, not to mention an independent-bodied adult. I am dating, too, something I never imagined when I was in a wheelchair and prone to spin out at any moment. Chalk one up to the elasticity of youth and the power of a quiet mind and living healthy! So when I say, 'Thank you, Pat, I owe you one,' I really mean that I've received a powerful gift from you."

"You don't owe me, Perlis," Pat said. "You really don't owe me a thing. Your becoming the man you are is enough. Your showing me—as you did just now—that you know the value of a gift and have the desire to serve is beyond enough. Taking the values you already know and living them, everywhere you go, with everyone you touch, more than expresses your gratitude. And when you live your values, you, too, will always have something to offer, not to collect people's gratitude but simply because situations arise where you are present with something to offer.

"Just one thing, Perlis," Pat added. "That's truly a remarkable story about the stone—what it said and what you learned from it. Until right now, I had never thought of a quiet mind as being so important to the way I lived. But I get it now. The message of the stone fits my life really well. When I saw you in the park, I was just moved by the situation unfolding around me, which I was a part of. I had a role to play that fit me really well. I took what felt like a spontaneous action in the situation, just out of interest in your and others' safety and well-being. When I saw you seizing, all my thought patterns—the ones that cycle continually and tell me, 'That's just the way of the world'—were quieted down. Being a human being and seeing another human being I could help was all that seemed clear. So I acted. And all my life since then, I've wanted to keep being available in every way to act like that."

26

As Pat finished speaking, Gene was experiencing the poignancy of the moment. Indeed, he realized that, if you looked at what Pat had done for Perlis—providing a means for him to eliminate conditions dangerous to his health—then indeed, Don had done the same for him. Gene felt blessed. A small tear appeared in the corner of Gene's eye, and he looked down, embarrassed to make eye contact with so much emotion running through him. Through misty eyes, a clump of brown dirt, pebbles, a dandelion, and what looked like uprooted grass came into focus. It was the clump of earth that Perlis had unintentionally kicked around like a soda can as he had ambled toward Gene and Pat. The clump, lying between Perlis and Gene and Pat, had not been moved since Perlis had come over to stand with them. It had been a silent witness to all that the trio had just shared. Gene then noticed that one of the pebbles was significantly larger than the rest and was sitting on top of the other pebbles.

Gene absolutely could not believe it. *How in heaven?* he thought. He could not deny it, either, though. There was an inscription on the surface of this largest stone in the clump.

"Look, guys!" Gene pointed, and Perlis and Pat gazed downward.

A passerby would have thought their next moves were synchronized. Their knees bent. Their shoulders rounded forward and they each extended a hand out and down toward the center point between them. The tops of their heads were within inches of each other, which caused a chuckle as they all reached down to pick up the stone. They raised their hands. Gene had the large pebble cupped in his right hand. Perlis's hand was cupped under Gene's. Pat's hand was cupped under Perlis's. It looked like a huddle among three men whose lives intersected. As they straightened to stand again, the shadows their bodies casted over the stone receded. Daylight reached the stone, and the words carved deeply and clearly on it were unmistakable:

SERVICE TO FELLOW HUMAN BEINGS

"Oh, my—does that reinforce what we were just saying, or what?" Gene asked.

"And what we're about to do," Pat said.

"You're about to do what? I'm coming!" Perlis declared.

"I've got an idea for you," Pat said excitedly. "Gene told me about something valuable that needs to be retrieved, and—crazy as I may be—I not only believe his story may be true, I am going to help him. I've accepted it as a True Security rescue mission. And you, Perlis, just might get more involved in this than you know. Come with us in Gene's car. He's driving the Corvair. We have a rendezvous in moments with some of our special equipment.

"And, oh, Perlis," Pat added. "You said you are a swimmer, right?"

"Yes, that's right, sir," Perlis answered.

"Do you have your swimsuit in your backpack?"

"Swim practice is this afternoon, so yes."

"Great, bring that."

Perlis shrugged his shoulders and thought, *OK*.

Gene pressed the gas as Middletown High School shrank in the mirror, Perlis in the front passenger seat, Pat filling both of their ears with precise instructions from the big, flat, beige backseat.

27

Pat and Gene, joined by an eager Perlis, arrived at the east bank of Riverbank Park, just upstream from the footbridge that rose over the river to their left. Gene restated to everyone that this was the place.

They heard the revving sound of a large white industrial vehicle powered by a strong diesel engine as a truck pulled up and then backed toward them. Looking closer, Gene saw that the vehicle had green-and-gold writing on it near the bumper. The stenciled letters read TRUE SECURITY UNIT 10. With the truck parked and the engine running, a man in a hard hat, wearing twenty-five pounds of gear, climbed down and introduced himself. "Chuck, unit captain, True Security Unit 10."

Rain in the distance meant heavier and faster-flowing waters were on their way. The river was already starting to rise. The time for the mission was now.

"Hardly time for introductions!" Pat yelled over the engine. "We're going to get this baby home, now!"

"Got that, sir," Chuck replied.

Pat and Chuck concluded that anyone wading into the water from the bank was liable to kick up a lot of mud with each footstep, blocking the view of the river bottom, compromising the retrieval of the valuable box. No one knew exactly what this "box" would look like.

"We're going to do this via descent from the bridge by crane arm. Who's willing to go for the ride, flight, *and* swim of your life?" Unit Captain Chuck asked.

"I am," Perlis said.

Chuck made eye contact with Perlis, then with Pat, then with Gene, waiting for confirmation of this offer. The lack of rebuttal gave him the desired confirmation. "Sounds good, kid. Here's your harness."

Out of the truck came their main special piece of rescue equipment, a cart the size of a boxcar rolling slowly on treaded tracks. It reminded Gene of a miniature version of the vehicle that had slowly carried the space shuttle to and from the launchpad. The prominent feature of this mighty cart was an arm that protruded from the front. Perlis sat closest to the front, then came Pat, and then Gene bringing up the rear. The three brave rescuers rode the slow-moving cart out onto the strong, cement footbridge. Chuck, the mission-control specialist, returned to the truck, keeping in contact via radio if necessary.

The time was here to share the physics of the mission, as Pat said to Perlis and Gene, "This 'little' cart weighs over seven hundred pounds. It is made of solid steel and iron, with a core of lead, and also clamps itself down onto whatever surface we park it on. It is the counterweight on the bridge, so no matter how much pull you exert as you extend out and descend down toward the water, your support will be stable up here. Importantly, we will always have the ability to pull you up."

Processing and mustering the courage for what he was about to do, without even knowing for certain—or even believing in--what he was looking for, Perlis gave a thumbs-up.

When the three on the cart were positioned on the bridge about fourteen feet over the water, they hooked Perlis's harness onto the extendable mechanical arm.

"Are you ready?" Pat asked excitedly, adrenaline pumping.

"Just like we planned!" Perlis responded.

"You can strap on your goggles now," Pat said, pointing to the headgear that was clasped to the left shoulder section of Perlis's full-body harness. "They're antifogging, my swimmer friend."

These headlamp-equipped goggles were to allow Perlis to keep his eyes open and see the river bottom. Attached to the goggles was an earpiece so Perlis could receive auditory information if necessary, even underwater, and a mini compressed-air tank and breathing regulator. It provided fifteen minutes of air and a five-minute backup supply. It was only used for brief dives.

After Perlis secured his goggles, the arm began to extend out from the bridge directly over the streaming water, taking Perlis with it, steadily, with a mechanical whirr, until it reached the desired extension.

"We're going to start lowering you. Remember to stay in dolphin position, with your hands, arms, and head pointed upriver and directly into the current, so you can stabilize yourself and hover above the river bottom," Pat said loudly, in the increasingly humid and breezy air under graying skies.

"Aye, aye!" Perlis said and saluted.

"Good luck, Perlis," Pat shouted.

Gene, not knowing what else to do, had been busy calling Hope on his cell phone, inviting her to "Get down here!" which she had quickly done. She stood just up the riverbank, watching in amazement. She had told Gene that Jim and Dana were both in class, but that Jim had said, "Whatever Dad's doing, tell him to be careful."

Meanwhile, Gene was actually praying. He wasn't sure what words to say, but most of all, he was feeling hopeful (and responsible) for the well-being of the teenager dangling over the water from the bridge.

"I've got you guys as my health advocates and warriors—I'm protected!" Perlis assured them.

Perlis's words had a calming effect on Gene. Taking relaxing breaths also allowed Gene's mind a moment to notice that he hadn't been able to reach Don, Rima, and Nat.

Gene's attention then shifted to Perlis, who was harnessed in and being lowered toward the water. Pat signaled to Perlis to insert his breathing regulator. The gap of daylight between Perlis and the river contracted by the second.

As Perlis's teeth solidly gripped the regulator, his body began to disappear beneath the surface.

Perlis quickly found out that this dive was nothing like diving into the high school pool for the Middletown swim team. Keeping his body aligned head-on with the onrushing current without going into a spin was an ever-present challenge. Knowing what to look for, and what it would look like when he found it, was his goal. The headlamp didn't quite brighten the riverbed as he had imagined, partly because of the increasingly cloudy skies above. The goggles and light provided a narrower field of vision than he'd expected, and the river bottom was strewn with decaying leaves, pointy and thorny branches, and more.

Time ticked by quickly as Perlis continued to struggle for a position that would allow him to see—and reach for—the buried treasure. He wondered whether the sky was getting darker or the helmet light's battery power was draining away. Forward and back, left and right, he wandered. He began placing his rubber-gloved hands on the bottom to see if the texture of objects could give him any clues. He began to wonder if Gene's story was true.

More than fifteen minutes had gone by, which meant only the reserve air remained. He was at the end of the line, literally as well as figuratively. Perlis took a deep breath, which he knew would be one of the last of his search because of his dwindling air supply. An intuition then suddenly came to him. It was neither something he'd heard with his ears nor seen with his eyes, but he followed this hunch a little to the left, a little forward. There, he saw some underwater plants, which in the light from the headlamp showed especially beautiful green blooms. Some small fish, brown ones and brilliantly colorful ones, nipped at the verdant foliage. Perlis especially noted that the plants were all arranged around a rectangular shape about fifteen inches long. Atop the rectangle, nothing grew at all; it was just a blank space surrounded by vegetation on all four sides. When Perlis felt that blank space, it was different from the rest of the river-bed. It felt hard and solid. Perlis then knew he had found something.

Expecting the box's surface to be slippery, as river stones are often slippery with moss or algae, he prepared to carefully reach for it. He felt it was important to grab the box firmly on his first try, because disturbing or dropping the box meant it might slip away in the current or get buried under the riverbed. But instead of being slippery, the box was almost magnetically attracted to his hands, clinging like static and adhering easily and effortlessly to his gloves. It rose out of the ground without resistance, as though weightless. The underwater plants growing out of the mud remained undisturbed.

And then, with the box in hand, Perlis rose.

28

As Perlis rose and breached the surface, Pat and the rescue team knew it was time for them to take over the mission. They reversed the direction of the crane arm, and the torque of the rescue device began to pull Perlis up by the harness despite the stiffening wind. All he had to do was hold on to the box tightly.

The professionally trained True Security Unit 10 crew made easy work of lifting and withdrawing the crane arm, despite the now-inclement conditions. Within moments, Perlis had returned safely to the bridge and was again sitting in the iron cart. No longer needing his breathing regulator and goggles, he removed them.

"You're a hero!" Pat beamed, patting Perlis's back.

"You've got a natural talent for rescue diving," Gene added.

Perlis, animated from the excitement, said, "That was amazing! I can't believe it! We got it; all three of us showed we could do it!"

The cart reversed direction deliberately off the bridge. Gene asked Perlis if he could hold the box, offering to trade him a towel to dry off with. Perlis assented gladly.

Finally Gene, Perlis, and Pat made it off the bridge and onto the riverbank. They stood and watched in appreciation for safety and rescue technology as the superheavy cart crane rolled back up the ramp into True Security Unit 10's truck. The box was slowly drying in Gene's hands, and Hope responded to Gene's expression and came to his side. Everyone squatted or took a seat on the pebbled riverbank.

On the box's lid was an inscription that read, in cursive, *The Seven Stones*.

"Gene, do you think Don and Rima are coming?" Hope asked. "I bet they'd *love* to see this!"

Gene answered, "Gosh, I hope so. I called them and left a message for them. They haven't been in touch yet."

He paused and then said, "Well, I'm finding out what's inside this box. We can show them when we get home. I still can hardly believe there was a box there, right where I saw it."

"Honey, I know," Hope agreed. "If you want to open the box now, I'm with you."

"'The Seven Stones,'" Gene repeated as he read the inscription. "This is absolutely incredible. Let's see what we have in here," he said with a shake of the box. The box didn't make a sound. Gene felt its solidity, especially toward the bottom. That must have been what kept the box solidly on the river bottom despite all the swift and changing currents flowing by.

As Gene removed the lid, the clouds released a bolt of lightning over the hills, and a booming thunder rumbled through the atmosphere. Inside the box, a purple ceramic bottom was revealed, with indentations in a pattern.

All the outer indentations were empty. The center indentation contained a stone. It was still slightly covered in mud, but it felt good to hold in the hands.

Picking up the stone, at first as though to make sure it was real, Gene felt its rough and curved surface as he gazed upon it. Like the stone Hope had found in the drawer, it was tannish red and sandstone-like, and perhaps a little heavier than one might expect given its size.

As Gene, Hope, Perlis, and Pat read the stone's inscription, it began to penetrate the layers of their understanding:

These are The Seven Stones. They offer you sacred practices to make a part of your lifestyle. When you live them, you become lived by them. Use the Seven Sacred Practices as guides for your healing, your wellness, and your growth as a human being.

Hope said, "There is something meaningful about the message being in stone and not on paper. It is as though it is being suggested to us, 'Give this message some time; it will not wear out. This message is time-tested.'"

Hope went on, "I mean, think about it! Stones last. Ancient buildings all around the planet that still stand today are made of stone. I am getting the feeling that we are going to be seeing value and meaning in these stones for quite some time."

In awe, and wet and chilly, they all stood around without speaking a word for a long, pregnant moment. Perlis was the first to verbalize it. "Wait, wait, wait, everybody—we've all been finding stones, right?" he exclaimed.

"I know, that's even more amazing, given that we've found this box," Gene said.

"I have mine; I always keep it in my backpack," Perlis said. He unzipped a pocket at the front of his pack and pulled out the Quiet Mind stone. "I really feel that I should place it right here," he said, gently placing it in one of the perimeter indentations inside the box.

"And I have three!" Gene bellowed. "Food, Air, and Water for Life Force; Physical and Mental Exercise; and Service to Fellow Human Beings. Here they go, into their rightful spots."

Hope then spoke up, coyly. "Well, let me just say, I've got a surprise for you at home."

"That's gotta be our next stop then," Gene said enthusiastically.

"Um, listen, I think the best thing I can do now is get to swim practice. I feel like I might break a record if I get in the pool now, I am so charged up!" Perlis said.

"I'll take you there, kid," Chuck said from behind them, farther up the slope of the riverbank. "Hop into True Security Unit 10."

"Thanks, Chuck! Talk about rolling up in some wheels, dang! I'd better call that cute girl on my team and ask her to meet me outside the natatorium! But before I go…you guys, Gene and Pat, I don't know what to say—you inspire me! Seeing what your lives are about, and what you came here to do, and my getting to be a part of it—you changed my life for a second time. I got to be part of retrieving a mysterious object and helping solve a puzzle that can give us a healthier future,, a puzzle that's still being solved. This whole adventure was far out. When I was dangling on the harness underwater I got to experience what it's like to go beyond the limits of our comfort zone to serve others."

Perlis continued, "Pat, today I not only got to meet and thank you for helping change my life, my health, and my worldview long ago; I also got to bond with you. I mean, together, we are allowing other people to access the Three Foundational Principles for Health and what the box seems to say will eventually be revealed as the Seven Sacred Practices. It's amazing to think that everything that's been happening at Riverbank Park might expand to benefit the whole world…Of course, what if we only find six stones?"

Pat and Perlis hugged before Perlis had more to say.

"Gene, Gene, Gene—out of the coma and into the mystic—you the man! Thank you for bringing awareness of the Three Foundational Principles for Health. They feel so fresh—I mean, they became clear to you today, and today you shared them at our school. I'm going to take them deep into my mind, and who knows, maybe chisel them in some marble or iron or something."

Gene and Pat laughed heartily at Perlis's suggestion.

"It's been more than an honor to meet you and get to know you," Gene said. "By the way, I'll take my son to one of your swim meets sometime this year. I look forward to introducing you to Jim. Feel free to call me to talk about plans for your adventure—the one coming up after graduation—wink wink. Take good care, Perlis."

Pat was in tears as he made eye contact with Perlis. He smiled warmly for nearly a minute, taking in how deeply Perlis understood and how young and promising he was for the world's well-being. "Pass it on, brother," he whispered with a heart-to-heart hug that left them truly feeling their brotherhood.

"Well, off I go," Perlis said, striding away and waving to Gene and Pat as he climbed up next to Chuck in the solidly built True Security Unit 10 truck. When he got in, Chuck slapped Perlis's back and said, "Tell that girl of yours I'll give her *and* you a ride in here."

"Really?" said a thrilled Perlis.

"Uh-huh—on the day she lets me know about her gifts to people and the planet's health and safety, I'll be waiting."

"All right…I see. I'll be sharing that," Perlis replied.

"Pat told me something about the principal—Jake, I think his name is—dragging his feet somewhat with safe and healthy school policies like only whole, unprocessed food, GMO-free and free of industrial slaughter and CAFO factory farming," Chuck said. "Maybe you and her can keep planting seeds in Principal Jake's mind."

Perlis replied, "I like where you're going with this, Chuck, my man!"

Still outside, Pat said to Gene, "OK, big man, I'm getting in the same truck as those guys. I've actually got a meeting to attend. I'm the speaker at a networking dinner for growing midsize companies that are looking to provide for their employees' and customers' needs for wellness and security. Oh…and I started the networking club. It's called Providing True Security and Wellness. It's a niche for us. What do you think?"

"As always, my friend, you are onto something ahead of your time," Gene said, smiling, with a slight shake of his head. Then he looked directly at Pat and said, "Keep it up."

"I will. And you let that woman love you," Pat said, gesturing toward Hope.

"You know I will," Gene said gratefully.

With slaps on their upper backs, Gen and Pat embraced. Then Pat hustled toward the True Security truck and climbed in, and the truck drove up the riverbank and departed, its rumbling engine rolling and fading away from Riverbank Park like distant thunder.

Hope, upon hearing the truck's roar fade, ambled back up from the water's pebbly edge where she'd been feeling the water ripple between her toes. She and Gene held each other's gazes, about three feet away from each other. Gene extended his left hand in Hope's direction, and she reached out with her right to hold it. In the many times they had stood near this river in this park, surrounded by the familiar walnut trees, inhaling the fresh and moist, yet subtle smell of jasmine and assorted flowers, never had they felt more in love or more gratitude.

29

Upon arriving triumphantly at his house, Gene exclaimed, "You know what a man needs? A man who gets out there and lives? I need a bath!"

It was the exultant shout of a man of action after a day when he had felt energetic, purposeful, and had been exerting himself. Even though he had a prosthesis, it simply hadn't mattered. He had been in motion that day, free of impediments to his energy, his body, or his mobility. And that was highly pleasurable.

Upon hearing what Gene had shouted out, Hope smiled. "I had a feeling you would say that."

"Oh, yeah? You think you finally have me figured out, after three decades of marriage?" Gene asked, laughing and sure-handedly placing the carefully cleaned Seven Stones box onto the living room coffee table.

"Come into the bathroom and let me show you how well I know you," Hope tempted Gene.

Ten beeswax candles had been placed all around their large bathtub. Warm bath towels fresh out of the dryer sat nearby, neatly folded. Epsom salts and Dead Sea salt awaited. Hope turned on the tap, starting the flow of steaming hot water, and then she lit the candles.

"What a great surprise! Thanks for knowing just what I needed, honey," Gene said.

"Today, you are acting on what I want, too, darling," affirmed Hope.

After taking off his prosthetic foot and leaning it against the bathtub, Gene sank his body into the filling bathtub. His muscles, ligaments, and bones began to relax. "Ahhhhh," he said. "Say, where in the house did you find the Food, Water and Air for Life Force stone?"

"In the kitchen drawer; my finger brushed it," Hope said.

"Amazing. How are they being placed so clandestinely in our lives?"

"Your guess is as good as mine, Genie. Hey, how do you like the temperature of the bath, sweetheart? It's pretty steamy."

Gene replied, "It's perfect. This candlelit environment, the minerals in the water, all of it is so rejuvenating. Give me another high school gym full of kids, I'm ready to speak…and then lift some weights with those young'uns! Long as you help lift me out of the bathtub, darling!" Gene added with a smirk.

"You're such a comedian, mister," Hope said. "Next you'll want a machine arm and a harness—but, as we see, unbelievable things happen."

"Are you coming in?" Gene asked, as Hope proceeded to massage Gene's shoulders from the end of the bathtub.

"I'll let you enjoy this one. After all, someone has to help you out," she said with a wink.

As Gene stood, he and Hope both reached for the fluffy towel at the top of the pile.

The sensation stopped them both cold. In the candlelight, they could see their pupils dilate further as their sensory nerves told them what had just been found.

"Another stone!" they shouted.

"Wow! OK…" Gene said, appreciating the "trick."

Hope couldn't contain herself. "Let's read it. What does it say?"

Under the glow of a candle, Gene and Hope saw the inscription on this stone read:

NATURALISTIC HYGIENE AND PROTECTION

"How interesting!" Hope said. "What this means, to me, is that things like bathing and warm human touch aren't just a reward for having a super day—they are something to be done, intentionally and consciously, as a sacred practice, one of the seven."

As if seeking extra credit from the Naturalistic Hygiene and Protection stone, Hope had prepared a mixture of shea butter and coconut oil, which Gene spread on his skin (the largest organ of the body), and hers. It created a youthful infusion to their skin cells, moisturized naturally, had an antiseptic effect, and was all-around medicinal.

Hope returned the favor, spreading the balm copiously on her beloved's skin till she got to his face. She looked him in the eyes, and before bursting into seductive laughter, her lips softly, gently, and slowly enunciated to him, "Naturalistic...Hi, Gene..."

Looking at him coyly for one more moment and batting her eyelids, she added, "And protection..."

30

The Curtin lovebirds kept their curtains open that evening at dinnertime, soaking in the view of the clearing storm clouds, revealing a pink dusk sky. As they came to the dining table, they had two things on their minds besides overwhelming awe at their day and the mystery of the box on their coffee table.

The first was the anticipation of sharing an intoxicating meal. Hope had briefly spent some of her morning prepping live sauces, like a creamy pecan marinara, and soup, a basil-mint-coconut-asparagus broth.

Intentionally, Hope had left an easy mixing task still to be done just before eating. One sensual way to mix this dish together could be to use bare hands—which, for the ingenious, forward-thinking Hope, was another benefit of having had Gene bathe his body, including hands, in minerals and organic soaps.

The second thought was the question, Where on Earth were Don and Rima? Certainly not returning their phone call.

"Oh, I'm sure they're all right. Maybe they just went on a trip and didn't tell anyone," Hope mused.

"Totally not concerned," Gene said. "Like you, just curious."

Letting the thought of their neighbors pass, Hope said, "Genie, want to hear the philosophy behind the live food dinner you will soon see before you?"

Gene certainly did. First, because he was hungry, and second, because earlier in the day, he'd told hundreds of kids that he wanted to find his path to life-supportive living, and as a grown-up he felt accountable to his word. "Well, yes. And plus, lunch was great, so more, please!"

"Sweet." Hope smiled. "I took the Three Foundational Principles for Health—cellular replacement, body consciousness, and perpetual motion on the whole-health creative continuum—and overlapped them with one of the Seven Sacred Practices: Food, Water, and Air for Life Force.

"Basically, we want healthier, more electrically charged and more vital cells to replace the cells that die every day—cellular replacement. We do this because we're aware of what our body's physical processes and tissues are going to do with what we feed it—body consciousness. And we want to move naturally; in your case, from a recovering diabetic physiology that still has some symptomatic days into a physiology that is stable in blood sugar, low A1C, diabetes-free, feels great, high strength and endurance, loving life. In my case, I want to keep my best energy levels, figure, skin, and mental clarity—whole-health continuum."

"Hey, Hope, that makes a lot of sense!" Gene said. "So, what are we eating?"

"Wait no longer, sweetheart," she replied.

She delicately pulled away the peach-colored tablecloth to unveil what it had been disguising. First to be seen was a piercing red-and-white, sprouted flax-and-nut-crust pizza bearing the brightest tomato sauce Gene had ever seen, and smothered with macadamia-sunflower cheese.

As she pulled the cloth away further, it revealed sprouted chickpea and raw avocado-oil hummus spread onto collard and romaine greens, topped with a peppery za'atar salsa fusion.

When Hope pulled the cloth off a large heap, the live basil-mint-coconut-asparagus soup, warm to the touch, appeared with a wood stirring spoon beckoning.

As the cloth was finally lifted off the table completely, a swirl of colors was seen bursting out of a bowl of blues, reds, greens, oranges, purples, yellows, blacks, and whites—a glorious rainbow salad full of vibrance.

"Oooh...Hope, you made all this? I'm the luckiest guy in the world!"

Squeezing a fresh, intoxicating lemon into the large salad bowl and a half teaspoon of unprocessed sea salt, Hope then touched Gene's hand. "Ravish our salad together, honey," she implored.

She showed him what she had learned from some videos and having an online chat with a raw food coach. "We're going to mix and massage this salad. It makes it more digestible, chewable, and agreeable to the taste once the lemon permeates the leaves."

Gene, recognizing his hands were as clean as they ever would be, his shirtsleeves were short, and that Hope had prepared perfectly, placed his hands in the bowl and followed Hope's lead. They began to knead kale, shredded carrot, purple cabbage, chopped cilantro, and diced tomatillo. Juice from each vegetable burst into their palms. Chunky, bulky masses shrunk down into rich, forest-green and rainbow edibles before their eyes. Their hands, more lathered in lemon juice by the second, found each other.

They raised their hands palm to palm out of the salad, in pantomime position but touching, giggling.

"Let's wash and sit down," Hope whispered. They, along with their fresh live food, were ready to eat.

They sat, inhaled and exhaled their great, sincere gratitude, served each other, picked up their forks, and ate this simple, bounteous symphony.

"Whoa, Hope, this is good," Gene said, slurping the pesto-mint broth. They sat there taking in the experience, from the spark of deliciously sour lemons, to the chlorophyll power packs of the leaves, to the deep, primal vigor of the sprouted seeds. Gene and Hope felt themselves light up! The nutrifying energy entered and expanded through them. They breathed, felt grateful to all whose hands this meal had passed through, the living Earth it all came from, and intentionally breathed the storm-cleansed air throughout their meal.

As they ate, Gene said to his wife, "Having this marvelous dinner, I had a flashback to my synesthesia experience."

"Really? I've been wanting to hear more about that. It's fascinating," Hope said earnestly.

Gene's face lit up as he forked some juicy, lemony rainbow salad. "Ah! Yes, now I get it. The sacred practice of Food, Water, and Air for Life Force is about vibration! That's why this meal has a look that's similar to what I saw this morning. Food and water carrying life force—that's what I've been able to see. And you're feeling that connection, too. I reckon it's what ultimately led you to learn and take the action to prepare meals like these."

As he nibbled on the tip of a slice of live pizza, Gene continued, "It seems this connection also relates to how it's possible that this box we retrieved can be, miraculously, sitting in our living room, as we speak."

"I know what you mean, Gene," Hope said as she poured herself some more coconut soup. "This is like a story out of *Unsolved Mysteries*, but for two differences—first, it's not on TV, and second, we're not as clueless as the narrator assumed us to be. I'd say we have a pretty good 'experiential education' about these things now."

"Sure," Gene said, shoveling a collard-avocado taco. "I'd like to review some of our 'experiential education.' I woke up invigorated after Jim and Dana were here and we heard how our neighbor, Rima, healed. She achieved the 'impossible,' but here she was, demonstrating and explaining it in as much detail as possible. Then, I'm walking in our park at daybreak, and suddenly I start 'seeing' the sound of the river. It was 'talking' to me. It 'told' me to look in a very specific place—within view of our most romantic spot in the city.

"Soon I'm talking to my former acquaintance who became a nutrition, wellness, and security celebrity superhero. He and the very kid whose life he changed forever, years ago, emerge together from a Middletown High School assembly to reveal themselves as heroes again for us in the uniform of True Security, Inc. And this evening, we're sitting here eating a bioenergenic meal based on a hyper-expanded understanding of how to heal ourselves and sustain our whole health.

"And possibly the weirdest thread running through it all? Our transforming paradigm is, get this, based on a well-fashioned and well-preserved treasure trove of engraved stones that these people have been finding for years before giving them to us, or that we've found ourselves. We don't know their source. Their message doesn't give away whether they're centuries old or from modern times."

"Yup," Hope said, flabbergasted, her animated eyes wide open with intrigue, her salad fork with rainbow greens suspended in mid-air in front of her.

"Hot dang, that's a lot to chew on!" Gene reflected, chewing more pizza.

They basked in the secrets they had yet to solve and the vital realities they were realizing nonetheless.

"Genie, speaking of chewing," Hope said after a moment, "I love you, and though I sincerely pray from my heart there will be many more, please consider this dinner the one I never got to serve you on the evening of your accident."

"Mmm," said Gene, chewing and digesting. "Definitely."

31

"How did you make this crust? God, woman, what a remarkable meal!" Gene said, as if it were his final bite. And then he took another.

"Sure you're done, or does the growing boy want some more?" Hope teased.

"I can't answer you, I'm chewing," he replied with his oncoming smile full of marinara sauce.

"Lovely. But I know what you mean. Mmm-mmm! I haven't enjoyed a meal like that since…I can't remember!" she squealed.

"Let's go visit Don and Rima," Gene suggested. "Bring them a container of soup and a couple slices of pizza or romaine wraps. Do they even know about today? I'd like so much to share it with them."

The stars were coming out as the sun retreated to the western horizon. Calm prevailed in the atmosphere after the storm's clearing. Gene hardly noticed his prosthesis as he walked; his mind dwelled on other, livelier notions. Hope marveled at her connection to Gene, to her body, to the ecosystem, to the forces and electromagnetic fields of nature that brought storms and clearings, thunderous atmospheric charges and bolts of lightning, dryness and rain, light and dark, heat and cold, and so much more.

As they strode unhurriedly in a bubble of love, toward the house two numbers up and across the street, that part of the neighborhood seemed quiet. At Don and Rima's house, the garage was closed and no lights were on. A gated porch led to the front door.

"It seems like nobody's home," Hope said.

Gene rapped on the door.

Silence.

"Did they say anything to you, Gene?"

"Not since they left our house last night."

Gene became curious and noticed there was a screen door in front of their front door. The screen door had both a doorknob and a bolt with a handle. He decided to turn the doorknob.

At Gene's lightest touch, the back of the doorknob and some loose screws plummeted and clanked inside the still-dark house. The sounds were muffled but still piercing in the nighttime silence.

The screen door slowly swung outward, creaking, until it was partway open.

"Hey, Hope! I just turned the doorknob and the front part of it spun off into my hand. It's a 'booby doorknob,' an extra."

"What...?"

"Yes, it's in my hand. And the screen door effortlessly opened."

"How extremely odd," Hope said.

"There's still the main front door here, behind the screen door," he said, opening the screen door fully and groping in the darkness to find the main door by raising his palm and pressing it forward.

"Here's the door." He was interrupted by a much deeper *creee-aaaaak* as the solid front door opened at the slightest pressure of Gene's palm.

"Is that the door opening, Genie?" Hope asked nervously.

"Indeed. All seems quiet; I think we're OK," Gene replied.

"My goodness, this is weird!"

After a pause, Gene spoke up. "Do you feel like we're supposed to go in? I kinda do. I sorta feel invited in; do you know what I mean?"

"Gene, I hope everyone's OK. I mean, where are they?" Hope asked, shivering.

Gene looked at Hope as she stood on the porch. "I know. I have a feeling that going through the doorway will clarify things." He turned back to the dark, open door.

"Hope, I'll take a step in and feel around for a light switch. Just because the lights are off doesn't mean they can't be switched on. If

Don and Rima are home and we disturb them, I'll just explain…I'll say that we sensed something and then heard something, and were feeling concerned."

"Hmm. OK, I'm with you, rain or shine," Hope said.

Secure in their decision and resolved to enter the house and find out more, Gene pressed on through the door, balancing himself on his left, biological foot and placing his right, prosthetic foot onto the first tile of the front hallway.

As he reached in to feel for a light switch, he found a row of them. He flipped the first one he felt, and nothing happened.

With his anxiety rising, Gene found himself praying internally. *May they be OK; may no harm have come to these friends of ours.*

He was ready with his finger on the second switch and flipped it up.

Light flooded the entranceway and illuminated the front of the house from the foyer to the den. Gene took in the situation as his eyes grew wide, swallowing hard.

"Oh, my, Gene, what?" Hope said from outside.

"It's essentially…" Gene leaned, bent, and swayed, and then walked a few steps in different directions. "Come in, Hope! It looks like it's totally…vacated!"

"What?"

"I don't know how this can be, but there's not a trace of anyone," Gene declared, circling back to the front door to escort Hope inside. "Everything's well lit, but it's furnitureless, pictureless, carpetless, and I think there's no china in the kitchen, either. Come in, have a look for yourself."

Hope took Gene's hand and stepped inside. After helping her in, Gene faced forward again, confronting this house-size mystery. Hope, however, took only one step into the house, stood still, and observed everything from that vantage point. She gazed down, and just to the left and an inch in front of her shoe was one of the pearlescent green earrings Rima had been wearing.

151

"Genie! Look—remember?"

Chills coiled up and down their bodies. "Look at the pattern. We saw it once on Rima's ear and thought it looked like a sun with seven planets!" Hope said, mesmerized by the evidence. "Do you recognize the shape now?"

Dumbfounded, the two, who had been through a remarkable journey that day, leaned toward each other and embraced. Tears welled in their eyes. Who were Don and Rima? They had never had friends like them before.

And now, they had gone as suddenly as they'd arrived. Gene hugged Hope close, the only thing he could think to do in this moment, missing his friends, uncomprehending—and if they were gone, grateful for the time they had had.

As he held Hope closely and firmly, Gene noticed that he was still holding the doorknob from the front of the house. It happened to be close to his eyes as his arms wrapped around Hope's head and neck, and the doorknob was turned at a particular angle to Gene's face.

"Wait! Hope, look what the doorknob is made of."

"Let me look," she said, craning to see. Gene dropped his arms and freed their hands.

"The part of the doorknob that we actually turn in our hands... it's a stone!" Gene practically shouted. Exhaling, then inhaling, he continued, "Good God! These people are just...not your normal people! How did they know we'd come here?"

"Do you think it's a message for us?"

In the silence after that question, they saw how to release the stone from its setting in the doorknob frame itself, which was a finely sanded and polished wood. After unfastening the stone from the wooden part of the knob, they were able to flip it over to find the previously hidden surface.

The stone faced them. It had boldly engraved words:

CULTIVATE RADIANT JOY

Gene and Hope read it together.

"That's what that exuberant feeling at dinner was," Hope said to Gene.

"Yes, I felt it and saw it in you, too."

"Joy, when authentic, radiates. That's definitely what I felt. A message for us; of course—it's the Seventh Stone!" Hope said with an excited shriek.

Gene spoke with steady earnestness. "I know a joy I've never known after a day like today. I could only have received this message—cultivate radiant joy—after today, a day of discovery.

"That rascal must have known, because I think he planted a note on my windshield wiper with a red rubber band, to tell me some kind of discovery was coming. I had no idea how profound it would be. I have learned a new level of gratitude for my health and what it is to cultivate *and radiate* joy.

"It can really have an effect on people," he added.

Hope smiled. She knew he got it. "You're right. You know how we couldn't remember the last time we'd enjoyed a meal like that?"

"Yes. The truth is, if I had come home for dinner instead of getting in my accident, I probably wouldn't have known how to enjoy eating as much as I just enjoyed that meal with you," Gene vocalized at the same time he discovered it.

Hope offered, "And you, Mr. Curtin, have been absorbed in cherishing your day since you and I got home, which has affected my heart. I am so proud of you. I love you."

Gene took a deep breath, let it out, and grabbed Hope's hand.

"Done here?" he asked.

"Time to go back home," she agreed.

Gene faced the light switch panel contemplated them a moment, and flipped them to off.

The two stepped out of the house and saw their illuminated porch across the street.

They left the doors swinging, unlatched and free. Their creakiness played a song in the silent night.

The cool, fresh air ventilated all night into Don and Rima's former house, circulating into the neighborhood and beyond, the essence of how they had lived there and given of themselves to those in need of their service.

32

Sitting side by side on the edge of their king-size bed, Hope and Gene opened their bedroom windows to the great outdoors. The reading lamp illuminating their laps, Hope and Gene ruminated like gumshoes looking over their clues.

"So," Gene reviewed, "in a faux doorknob at Don and Rima's house, we found the Cultivate Radiant Joy stone, the seventh stone."

"Now Rima and Don have disappeared with the wind," Hope added.

"Wait, did you hear what you just said?"

"I said, really, did Don and Rima have to pull this doorknob-and-disappearance stunt just for us to find out..."

"Oh, my God!" they both shrieked.

"All the stones?" Hope claimed.

"Given by Don and Rima?" Gene finished the thought.

Hope nodded her head imperceptively as she said, "It's beyond understanding. How could it have been orchestrated? I could scarcely even begin to tell you how they could have done it..."

Gene was still examining the wooden part affixed to the Cultivate Radiant Joy stone. "It is a mystery hard to fathom. Let's see what else we have here, if there are any clues..."

The rest of the doorknob was made of a type of wood that looked familiar—although it lacked the water stains, it could have been the same wood that the Seven Stones box was made of.

Looking very closely, they were surprised to see an inscription etched in multiple rings that wrapped around part of the doorknob.

It read:

> By now, you have found the Seven Stones, and
> you have begun walking the path
> of the Three Foundational Principles for Health
> and the Seven Sacred Practices.
> Everything we could have told you,
> about ourselves and about well-being,
> we have finished telling. The practices
> are in how you live them and are lived by them and...

The inscription drifted off, unfinished.

As Hope and Gene looked up, feeling chills and a light sweat a whisker-thin meteor blazed above them in the sky. It left a glistening silver trail connecting their house to Don and Rima's house and extending far beyond.

33

Hope was up after a rejuvenating night of sleep before morning's light streamed in through the crack in the window shades. By the first clear sunbeam, she was warming up on the backyard wooden deck that Gene had constructed when they'd first moved in.

Gene was awake, too, carrying the Cultivate Radiant Joy stone from the bedside table to the Seven Stones box, which was on the living room coffee table. As he placed the stone into the box, he noticed something that confirmed what he had suspected yesterday. Although he hadn't been keeping count, now he was sure.

"Hope!" he called. "Why have you been calling last night's stone the seventh stone? There are six outer stones present here. There's still a vacancy among the seven outer indentations."

"Well, Mr. Gene Curtin, aren't you observant? You'll just have to believe me when I say I'm full of surprises," she teased.

"Is that right? Do tell," Gene said, playing along.

Hope picked up a glass of cold-pressed green juice, took a sip, and set it back on the deck. She continued, "You didn't know this, but yesterday morning after you'd left—and before Rima and Don, well, disappeared—guess who came over to say hello? Rima!"

"Oh, really?"

"Yes, and you know, we had some woman time together," Hope explained with a smile. "That's what makes their 'disappearance' so surprising. Although...if they knew they were going to vanish, it would make sense..."

"What do you mean? What would make sense?"

"Well, she brought over these mats, yoga mats. We came right to this spot and she taught me some things. We did over an hour of, well, stuff together. First we did some intentional breathing. I felt very, well, 'awake' after that. Then she showed me some movements called qi gong. And, Gene, I loved it! I felt tingly energy in my hands and between my fingers."

"Oh, so it sounds like you and I both had some interesting new experiences yesterday morning, you with the qi gong and breathing, and me with synesthesia at the rippling water," Gene said. "Ha—just a couple of days ago, would you believe we would be having this conversation? What changes!"

Hope went on, "All I know is I was ready for more. So Rima taught me a basic series of yoga movements. Boy, what a way to start the day!"

"Don't tell anyone I said this, but...can you teach it to me?" Gene asked.

"Of course, sweetie! So," Hope's voice grew more excited, "let me tell you how it ended. From what I've put together, this was right during the time you were having the synesthesia."

"I'm certainly listening. Watch out—I might see your words in colors and lights."

"Very funny! So, we complete our yoga movements, and Rima tells me that it is important that we lie down on our backs, return our breathing to completely normal, feel our core, and give our nervous systems the opportunity to integrate a new body awareness from the series of movements we've just done. So even though it seemed like I had just gotten out of bed, I just lay back down as I was asked.

"After a while on our backs, Rima asked me to sit up comfortably, scan my body, and continue to be aware of my breath. So I did. I liked being attentive to my body and my breath. I began to feel quite... present. Feelings of gratitude arose spontaneously," Hope revealed.

"So you and Rima were meditating—can we call it that?—while I has experiencing synesthesia, which had never happened before. That very synesthesia led me to see lights that, in my consciousness, identified where Rima's husband, Don, may have buried a box for the Seven Stones, which he also surreptitiously placed all around in our lives?" Gene said incredulously.

Hope was overflowing with awe, saying, "Not only that, but before she left, Rima rolled up the yoga mats we were using and handed them to me. We can practice anytime we want now."

"Wow, there's an idea," Gene gently teased.

"Why wouldn't we? Look what it did for us yesterday," Hope said with a wink.

"Let me see that mat. Oh, so it's rolled up like a spool. What's this at the end?"

"I don't know, a cap or something, to keep it rolled up? By the way, try this green juice."

Hope was playfully feigning ignorance, as she had put two and two together after finding the first stone in the drawer the morning after the family study session. Sharp as an eagle, when she saw Rima enclose a small round object in the yoga mat, her heart told her to wait to unwrap it with Gene. To her, the box itself and the remainder of the carved stones that turned up elsewhere were unanticipated developments, but she had caught on enough to be patient and wait for Gene so they could discover the message of this stone as a couple.

"Delicious!" Gene exclaimed after trying the green juice. Then he continued, "Look at this cap; it's squeezed in tightly inside the spooled yoga mat. I can't pull it out while it's rolled up. As a mechanic, I'd say the mat is keeping the cap in place, rather than the other way around."

Hope's curiosity and excitement was piqued, just as she'd intended. "Unroll it, honey!"

Like unrolling a red carpet, Gene spread the yoga mat onto the deck while holding one end with his left hand. The mat completely unfurled, leaving an unrecognized object sitting at its center. It didn't immediately look like a stone. Whatever it was, Gene and Hope beheld an object covered in tissue paper with elegant, contoured handwriting upon it in fine green ink.

As though he was actually going to practice yoga, Gene got on hands and knees on the mat and read the paper covering the object. It said:

> To a lucky guy:
> This is one sure way
> To make sure you open your yoga mat.
> *Love Always*

"So sneaky!" Gene rumbled.

"Indeed! Those two!" Hope said. "Never mind, though, Gene—see if the tissue paper peels off…"

In a suddenly romantic mood, Gene crooned, "We've seen miracles this past weekend, Hope, and I know we're not done seeing them. We have received the miracles of food and water, physical and mental activity, quiet mind, offering service, naturalistic hygiene, and definitely lots of radiating joy. Hope, let's open this one together."

"Are you asking me to dance?" she demurred, fantasy achieved.

"Absolutely."

"I'd be honored, sir."

With Gene holding the stone in the palm of his right hand, Hope pinched the tissue paper between her thumb and forefinger and lifted the paper off of what would appear to be the final stone.

It was a lovely, rounded beige stone with limestone-like patterns strewn through it. The inscription said one word only, simply:

ENERGETICS

Their eyes scanned it silently, quizzically.

"Could energetics be how you and I were connected yesterday morning, both having our experiences at the same time?" Gene asked.

"And could energetics be how both us 'old ponies' are up doing yoga early in the morning after a relaxing night of sleep?" Hope pondered.

"Yeah, um...and drinking this green juice. What's in here, anyway?"

"Vegetables and Chinese and Ayurvedic herbs, that's all," came Hope's kittenish answer.

"How did I know you would say something like that?"

"Energetics!" Hope said boldly.

Now getting into it, Gene went on, "And tell me, lovely lady, why do I have a feeling that yoga and green juice are going to be part of our lives, happily ever after?"

"Energetics!" they whooped together.

34

Jim and Dana were married the next summer, the same summer Gene's doctor declared him a miracle case of recovery from type 2 diabetes. One day in midautumn, Hope, who had completed a class in live, whole, plant-sourced nutrition and cuisine, was hanging a recently developed family picture from the summer's wedding, savoring the precious, irreplaceable togetherness and health of their family. For brunch, Hope served Gene a daikon, watermelon, and arugula salad with soaked and spiced almonds, topped with hard-to-find 100 percent pure unheated olive oil, turmeric dressing, and cayenne pepper.

"By missing one of your meals last year, Hope—you know the one—I learned a lesson that essentially earned me a second life, so I can now enjoy many, many more of your meals. I love that! They're better than ever, my dear, just like I love you more than ever," Gene bubbled.

An hour later, Gene was setting about his home improvement projects as the sun rose high in the sky. It was nearly noon. The season's raking was in full swing, leaving a pile of leaves in the backyard. He enjoyed the motion of raking a great deal. Like the whole-health warrior lifestyle, the activity of raking leaves was as much about the process as the result. The leaves always fell from tree branches; the task, and its required attention, was never, ever finished. The raking motion involved rhythmic weight transfer between his feet and legs, a lot like swinging a baseball bat. He was feeling the almost-sensual pleasure of the activity and gratitude for his functioning and healing body, when all of a sudden he heard a sound that he doubted a leaf could make under his rake.

Ting!

One tine of his garden rake again made a tiny, barely audible *clang* against something in the leaves.

He remembered learning from Don and Nat that sometimes the answer you are looking for is where you wouldn't have thought to look before, because it was hard to see there.

Gene got into a squat, set the rake aside, and shoved his right arm into the center of the pile of leaves, noticing that his hand and forearm disappeared all the way past his elbow. Feeling along the ground, eventually he found it—a hard little object. Gene grabbed it in his strong fist and withdrew his arm from the mountain of leaves.

It was a tool with a palm-fitting handle. It had one simple, useful feature, a straight and strong-looking iron projection. Its tip was a sharp wedge.

Into the wooden handle was etched, "Share Them."

Gene knew exactly what this was in reference to. He walked with energetic strides over to the garage, where he kept the doorknob. It was true that Don and Rima had never returned; they were truly gone with the wind.

"Hope, please come into my lair," Gene invited, sticking his head around the doorway to catch Hope's attention. "You'll want to see this."

The sharp object Gene had discovered in the pile of raked leaves moments ago was a carving tool, with etchings carved deeply into its well-worn handle, meant to endure through its passing from hand to hands—for as long as balance and wellness were sought by human-kind. The engraving read:

Having gathered the Seven Stones, and
begun walking the path of mastery
of the Seven Sacred Practices and the
Three Foundational Principles for Health,
discovering this tool confirms that

you are now the Whole Health Warrior,
the storyteller, the guide and the carver
entrusted with keeping the message of the Seven Stones clear.
The practices are in how you live them, are lived by them, and
share them.

—∿—

And so it continues. Far in the past, someone who had experienced the wisdom of the Seven Sacred Practices passed them on to Don and Rima. Don and Rima then passed them along to Gene and Hope.

Now, they are being passed on to you. Like Gene and Hope, you have uncovered the secret of the Seven Stones and the Seven Sacred Practices, which are the keys to whole-person health. You are now, and will be forevermore, a whole-health warrior.

Epilogue:
Mom, Memories, and My Children

In the late afternoon, a little before dusk, the sky was a shade of gray-blue in constant transition. Even though I had a house filled with my wife and our children, who were visiting from school, my thoughts were on the very recent passing of my mother.

Her uncommon death of the body occurred on a wildlife excursion that she had organized for herself and other senior women. Yes, an expedition at alpine elevations in the back hills, with my long lived mother acting as the fauna guide.

I knew very little about my mother's last day. She had already been out for four days on the journey into the wilderness. My perspective on the passing of Hope Curtin was limited to the view through the glasses of a mourning son. I felt a heavier *thud* in my stomach than I had ever felt before when I heard the news. From the unusual circumstances of Mom's death, it seemed that only her enduring vigor had enabled her to be camping at her age. *So, was her vitality her mortality?* I wondered.

After a week of grieving, consoling, and being consoled, I still didn't have the full picture of exactly what had happened. In my quest to know more, and to be there for my father as often as possible, I decided I would visit him again, even with Sara and Lara, my daughters, visiting from school.

I kissed Dana by the kitchen counter and, giving her soft left hand a squeeze, I said, "I'll be back from Dad's in a little while. You and the girls OK?"

"Sure, Jim, I understand. Maybe Sara, Lara, and I have visited Dad enough for now, and a little time with you and your dad alone would be good for you both. Besides, while the girls are still here for the weekend, we're doing a project together, trying out some new recipes: stuffed-tomato pâté and sea vegetable soup. We might be able to prepare enough food for the next couple of days, too."

"That sounds great. I think you're probably right about my going alone. I want to let him talk to me fully, as much as he wants."

"I love you, Jim," Dana said.

"I love you. Let the girls know I *will* be back for dinner."

Dana gave me a warm and reassuring peck on my cheek at the door as I stepped out into the cool air.

My father's house in those grassy hills was quiet compared to our city digs. Mom and Dad's place was the home of so many memories; it seemed odd, to put it mildly, that my mother no longer lived there. There was not a corner of this vast green planet where I could find my mom to talk to her face-to-face again. Not ever, not on this Earth.

I opened the squeaky garden gate, which, to my surprise, my father must have heard. Either he was waiting for me, or he had impressive hearing for a man in his eighties. Or both. In any case, I saw Dad approach through the transparent glass front door and flip the latch to unlock it.

Meanwhile, I heard my breath in the silence of that sparsely populated neighborhood as I treaded the walkway between the trellises for pea shoots that Dad was cultivating in the front yard. My shoes made a soft scraping sound on the groomed dirt trail between the garden gate and the front door.

What I noticed about my dad's posture and mood, even as he waited for me at the front door, was that he looked surprisingly at ease with himself, given Mom's recent death.

"Jim, nice to see you. How are you doing?" he asked.

"Glad I'm here, Dad. I need to be here, actually."

"Dana OK? And the girls?"

"I'm sure it's anything but easy for them, but what's there to do? We're all taking stock of Mom's life and love for us," I commented.

Then I felt it was important to add, "One thing we're doing is sharing everything with Sara and Lara. I want to protect them, of course, but Mom is—was—no, *is* their grandmother. I feel that we owe it to them not to hide anything. Death, they've got to know, is a part of life...but it's hard, Dad, you know? God, Mom lived a good, full life, didn't she?" I struggled to say, growing emotional.

Silence sat with us in the living room, the same living room that framed much of the book I have penned.

"Your mother told me recently, just before she went, that you had some kind of regret, that you think you didn't pay enough attention or something?" my dad said.

I thought to myself, *Amazing: my mom leaves this Earth, yet her concern for my well-being is still reaching me, through Dad.*

"Yes, I had told her that a couple of weeks ago while she was over—you know, when I realized it was time to show her the book, because..."

"Yes, yes, son. I know why."

"Do you really know, Dad? Do you really know what getting you back meant to me? To all of us? You had started dying. Passing out. Losing parts," I said, glancing toward Dad's foot and then back into his eyes with a mix of remembered agitation and present-day gratitude.

I continued on, "But you saw a different and new vision. You stopped killing yourself and essentially hurting us. The results, beyond you staying alive for us and yourself? Dana got to have you as a father-in-law—and *father-in-love*. Sara and Lara have you as a grandfather. And more!

"So yes, I asked Mom—as I have always wondered—was I too busy in my own life, meeting Dana and studying, to really have a perspective on what had been happening to you before the accident and what has been happening to you ever since, right up to this day?"

It was full dusk now, the valley's twinkling electrical lights coming into sharp resolution.

My dad said, "Jim, when I said you touched people with your writing, I meant to fully include your mother in that."

"Dad, c'mon, what did Mom need to be touched by the book for? She lived it," I insisted.

"I remember the way your mother gloated about having had the first opportunity to read what you wrote. As she explained it to me, she read it uninterrupted, except for drinking some, what was it, chai tea?"

"Yup." I smiled. "Brewed it myself."

"She told me every detail, son. She also said that reading your book cover to cover was broken up by only one other thing. She would briefly meditate with the book against her heart, so that she could call up her memories and let the power of those episodes in her life flood back into her."

"My goal was to transcribe the story accurately and tell it with feeling, so it's awesome to hear this," I said.

"Perhaps you have no idea what your writing meant to her. I'll tell you. Your book, son, let your mother see her actions—the fruit of her love and connection to life—live on beyond her. The night she came home and told me about your book, right before she fell asleep, she said, 'That book's going to make a difference for others. It has story, feeling, knowledge, and support.'"

"Really, Dad? That's a lot of what I was aiming for, but I didn't see much of a reaction from her. She just thanked me for letting her be the first to read it," I stated. And then, holding myself back from weeping, I said, "And that was the last time I saw her."

My dad's heavy eyelids blinked with both sorrow and understanding. "Well, son, in fact, it was due to Hope's massive response, in front of yours truly, that I sat down the next morning to start reading it, too. Sure, I read between pruning pea shoots and tomato vines and teaching my whole-health warrior classes, but I surely set to reading it. It turns out, I just reached the last page today."

"Just before I arrived?"

"Yup. And I confidently say to you, Jim—and I've seen a few things about human nature in my life—that you certainly paid close enough attention to be of a real service to the people out there who are waiting for your book. By not keeping this experience to yourself, but sharing it, you are touching people, guiding them toward the source of a healthier, more conscious life."

I had to reply, choked up: "Dad, maybe so. I mean, I am as happy to contribute to people's 'edutainment' as the next would-be author, but I still have my doubts as to whether I really conveyed the true message of what happened to you both, the courage you and Mom took on for life. And now that Mom's gone," I said, breaking into sobs, "it's like that again, Dad. I don't know how she died—exactly— and it matters. At least to me, it matters."

Dad just looked at me. His shoulders heaved with deep breaths, with loss and love, with the emotional extremes of the recent death of his wife and the nearby aliveness of his child.

"Jim," he said, "since you're asking...and since you feel it's best for not only you but also for your children to know everything, I can understand that."

I looked at my dad and my eyes said to his, *Thank you, Dad. Please do tell me.*

"I'm gonna tell you everything I know, Jim, as well as I know it... And hey, pay attention, will ya?"

"Ha-ha," I said, dense clouds of grief breaking up into a lighter and more diffused humor.

"Jim, do you know why I wasn't with Mom the last day she came over to your and Dana's place?"

"You were teaching your whole-health warrior public class series for seniors and retirees, right?"

"Yes, that particular day, it was on organic edible gardening for small spaces. Thus, Hope visited your place alone."

I said, "Yes, I knew that, and I remember thinking how cool it was that Mom was reading my book while you were out teaching and sharing what you'd learned from what happened. What's this got to do with Mom's wilderness trip?"

"Your mother and I got home at about the same time that evening, after she'd visited you. She was already beaming when I first saw her. It's interesting to me, son, that you say she didn't give you that much of a response about how the book affected her. That's so different from the exuberance she showed me," he said.

I could only repeat, "As I said, she thanked me and said that it represented the story extremely well. Just that."

"Well, she might not have wanted to clue you in to everything, given how closely you paid attention."

"I have a feeling I know where this is going, and I can see why she didn't tell me," I said, drying tears in the corners of my eyes.

"What sometimes happens when you recall important parts of your life," Dad said, "is that you relive them with the enrichment of present-time perspective. I trust you do sense where this is going. What can be said? Hope—Mom—remembered what she loved, second only to her family."

We both paused.

Then Dad continued, "So she packed her backpack. Jim, while on these camping treks, Mom especially loved to go off a little distance and allow thoughts of the largest kind to come through, clearing her mind of rigid constrictions. While away from the group for one such moment of solitude, Mom was sitting peacefully on a giant tree root that grew next to a stone crag. Sitting on this root and leaning on the stone, Mom had been gazing upon the gorges below and around her and listening to the sounds of leaves and the calls of animals. From that grand throne, Mom adjusted her footing and accidentally disturbed a green Mojave rattlesnake's underground home. Behaving naturally to protect its space, the snake struck your mother's inner right foot, injecting her with venom.

"Other ladies in the group—Trudy and Stella, I think were their names—found Mom's body almost an hour later, sitting, still warm, on the root of that tremendous cottonwood, continuing to exude a sense of deep peace. When she was found, Mom's back remained upright against the granite stone. Mom's slightly dusty face, still luminescent with beauty and wonder, bore a single trail from her eye down to her chin, showing the streaming path of a tear that had fallen at the moment of her end.

"And that's the extent of the detail, at the level I know it," he finished.

I said, "Dad, I think of her in that moment. Living her bliss in the wilderness, on a tree root, resting against solid stone. These were some of her favorite elements.

"Then she was bitten by a rattlesnake—where on her body? On the same foot that you lost. Once you were without part of your right foot, Mom helped all of us discover how to help you live.

"Mom must have been overjoyed about backpacking in the wilderness, at her age. And she could really observe, couldn't she? I wonder what she was observing at the moment she was bitten and decided, I assume, to stay seated rather than attempt to run for help? I'm coming to believe that Mom may have looked at the foot that had been bitten, and it called up her remembrance of life, her husband, her children, and her grandchildren.

"When I came over tonight, I was grappling with this thought that disturbed me about Mom's passing. I couldn't shake the feeling that Mom, and her death, somehow proved that life is like a zero-sum game. I looked at her demise during backpacking, an activity Mom did with such vigor, and the thought played in a repeating loop, 'Mom's vitality was her mortality.'

"Yet, then all in a rush, I remembered the qualities of *love* and *choice*. I looked as observantly as I could at what happened to her.

"Mom's vitality gave her not her mortality, *but the choice to die as she loved.*"

"Son, oh, my," my dad said, trembling slightly. "Now I know you paid good attention, for I have come to see her final day the same way."

"Believe me, I've examined the symbolism ad nauseam, Dad... well, ad nauseam until it became 'postnauseam.' By that, I mean it doesn't turn my stomach anymore, because...I have to say...I know it was for the best. I don't know any other way she could have died, because she was living the only way that fit her."

Dad just nodded. Save for his crops and flowers, he would be alone when I went home. Who could know what the future might bring for a man so recently and unexpectedly widowed?

"Jim, when you go," he said, anticipating my departure, "know that I'm all right. Hope amplified the love in my life a zillionfold. Especially the past twenty years, I knew love was an inside job. Actually, I couldn't have healed without realizing that. So although I am mourning, I am still connected to that feeling of the spiritual self that flows in me."

And for once, I had no doubt. I grabbed my jacket, which I'd taken off and laid beside me on the couch, tucked it under my arm, and indicated that I was going to take off, as my family was waiting for me. We hugged each other for a comfortable three breaths, a particularly sweet father-son embrace.

As I stood on the threshold, back out in the now-dark and almost-misty evening, Dad added, almost as if he was announcing it to all who would hear, "You know, speaking of that inner flow of being...your mom was quite a fountainhead, herself."

That *really* made me smile, and I grinned at my dad, piercing through my veneer of grief.

As I rounded the curve to leave Dad and get back to Dana and the girls, my mind cycled through my mother's life from my point of view as her son. At my age, my 50's now, having been living the Three Foundation Principles for Health and the Seven Sacred Practices for decades, I had a precious confidence that I would not be falling into a hypoglycemic coma while I drove. I still ate as I had learned to eat from my mother and father as a young adult when my parents were reclaiming their birthright to life.

My joints and feet, for which I give thanks, are no impediment to moving with ease. This fact I owe to the human and divine intervention that took place in my parents' lives and from which I learned. Yes, I did pay close attention, I realized. I saw that the proof was right in front of me: my drive across town to return to my family ended only in me successfully reaching home, with no blackout crashes then or in the foreseeable future.

As I pulled into my driveway and turned off the ignition, a new feeling arose in my heart. I felt Mom was completing her psychic good-byes. Her departure felt more final now, as if she was satisfied by the talk Dad and I had shared that evening. She felt free to go on her journey after seeing my power to nourish and protect myself and my family in good health of mind and body as I aged and "saged." He discoveries—those she absorbed from others and those made by trial and error—lived on. She sailed off into the light knowing this was among her greatest contributions, not only to her beloved family, but to her nearly equally beloved field of biology.

The fountainhead that was Mom was the archetype of the whole-health warrior, which now lived in my family's home, and it felt sacred.

I walked toward my front door, removed my shoes, and placed them in the porch shoe rack. I entered the front door knowing I was going to enjoy the raw rainbow root spiral salad dressed with a blend of sprouted sunflower seeds, tomatoes, oregano, thyme and sauce.

My beloved Dana, Sara, and Lara were just sitting down for dinner. As I entered the main family area of the house, my daughters' radiant smiles made my own face light up. When my gaze met Dana's, both of us said an eyes-open prayer:

May we be whole-health warriors. May we, now, be the new fountain of awakening, transformation, nutrition, holistic natural prevention, and healing for our present generation, as we have seen our elders courageously exemplify before us. May we realize life-sustaining, deep love, aliveness, and one-ness with all creation. May we, like our ancestors, live and die as called to by our highest vibration of consciousness.

The Seven Sacred Practices of the Whole Health Journey

Author's Statement

I have responded to a calling over the past decade to tell stories based on my observations, and discovered that doing so can help people. Noticing this has lent purpose to my qualitative and quantitative research. After extensive documentary and narrative film experience as early as college, I prepared to become a health and wellness coach and spiritual counselor. Central to the joy in my life is the practice of meditation and yoga. I am currently co-director of the East Bay Healing Collective, and co-leader of the Heart of Light Meditation group, which serves the San Francisco Bay Area. This gives me the capacity and venue to share teachings by other teachers, facilitators, and speakers as well as myself. It is an honor to have guided wellness and spirituality programs in many cities, and served as a guide and teacher at the Tree of Life Center US. I also co-founded Soma Naturals, LLC, which provides organic raw cleanses and juices, and am the director of Tree of Life – San Francisco and the Peninsula. I see myself as a voice helping to articulate the evolution of how people relate to one another; to eating; to ecosystems; to health; to personal power, freedom and responsibility; and to living creatures. Thank you for reading, and please, if you feel called, take this opporutnity to communicate with me.

For more information, please see:
www.readsweethealing.com and www.michaelbedar.com

This book's website—learn more and leave a comment:
www.readsweethealing.com

The author's website:
www.michaelbedar.com

The author's service and projects:
www.healingcollective.org
www.somanaturals.com
www.treeoflifebayarea.com

Close and direct help with *Sweet Healing: A Whole Health Journey*:
www.treeoflifefoundation.org
www.drcousens.com
www.wholehealthwarrioracademy.com

More resources for the reader and friends of the author:
www.thehealthylivingshow.com
www.lifefoodorganic.com
www.mayispeakfrankly.com
www.happyfornoreason.com
www.rawgourmet.com
www.rawfamily.com

www.debbiemerrillshow.com
www.fullyalivemedicine.com
www.cookingwithjia.com
www.markusrothkranz.com
www.naturalnews.com
http://programs.naturalnews.com
www.susansmithjones.com
www.bestmedia.com
www.pmcmarin.com
www.hippocratesinst.org
www.ravediet.com

Made in the USA
Charleston, SC
18 November 2015